The Last Days *of* New Paris

BY CHINA MIÉVILLE

The Last Days

of

New Paris

A Novella

CHINA MIÉVILLE

PICADOR

First published 2016 by Del Rey, an imprint of Random House,
a division of Penguin Random House LLC, New York

First published in the UK 2016 by Picador

This edition first published 2017 by Picador
an imprint of Pan Macmillan
20 New Wharf Road, London N1 9RR
Associated companies throughout the world
www.panmacmillan.com

ISBN 978-1-4472-9654-6

The image of the *Exquisite Corpse* by André Breton, Jacqueline Lamba, Yves Tanguy (1938)

Scc   15.

and all   ures,
a
Where   ogues
concern   events

Printed and bound by CPI Group (UK) Ltd, Croydon, CR0 4YY

Visit **www.picador.com** to read more about all our books
and to buy them. You will also find features, author interviews and
news of any author events, and you can sign up for e-newsletters
so that you're always first to hear about our new releases.

To Rupa

"One overhears many reactions to surrealist art, but the most pathetic of all is from those who ask, 'What am I supposed to see and feel from this?' In other words, 'What does papa say I may think and feel about this?'"

GRACE PAILTHORPE,
"On the Importance of Fantasy Life"

CONTENTS

The Last Days *of* New Paris

Exquisite Corpse by André Breton,
Jacqueline Lamba, Yves Tanguy (1938).

Chapter One

1950

A street in lamplight. Beyond a wall of ripped-up city, the Nazis were shooting.

Past the barricade and a line of tailors' mannequins assembled in a crude and motionless cancan, Thibaut could see the khaki of scattering Wehrmacht men, gray dress uniforms, SS black, the blue of the Kriegsmarine, all lit up by the flares of weapons. Something sped along the rue de Paradis, weaving in a howl of rubber between bodies and ruins, coming straight at the Germans.

Two women on a tandem? They came very fast on big wheels.

The soldiers shot, reloaded, and ran because the

rushing vehicle did not turn or fall under their onslaught. There was a whir of chains.

Only one woman rode, Thibaut made out. The other was a torso, jutted from the bicycle itself, its moving prow, a figurehead where handlebars should be. She was extruded from the metal. She pushed her arms backward and they curled at the ends like coral. She stretched her neck and widened her eyes.

Thibaut swallowed and tried to speak, and tried again, and screamed, "It's the *Vélo*!"

At once his comrades came. They pressed against the big window and stared down into the city gloom.

The Amateur of Velocipedes. Lurching through Paris on her thick-spoked wheels singing a song without words. *My God,* Thibaut thought, because a woman was *riding* her, and that absolutely should not happen. But there she was, gripping the Vélo's wrist with one hand, pulling with the other on leather strapped tight around the cycle-centaur's throat.

The Vélo moved faster than any car or horse, any devil Thibaut had yet seen, swaying between the façades, dodging bullets. She tore through the last of the men and the line of figurines they'd arranged. She raised her front wheel and hit the barricade, mounted the meters of plaster, stone, bone, wood, and mortar that blocked the street.

She rose. She hurled into the air above the soldiers, arced up, seeming to pause, falling at last through the invisible boundary between the ninth and tenth arrondissements. She landed hard on the Surrealist side of the street.

The Vélo bounced and twisted on her tires, slid sideways. She came to a stop, looking up at the window of the Main à plume's hideout, straight into Thibaut's eyes.

He was first out of the room and down the splintering steps, almost falling from the doorway out into the darkening street. His heart shook him.

The passenger was sprawled on the cobbles where her mount had bucked. The Vélo reared above her on her hind wheel like a fighting horse. She swayed.

She looked at Thibaut with pupil-less eyes the same color as her skin. The manif flexed her thick arms and reached up to snap the cord around her neck and let it fall. She rocked in the wind.

Thibaut's rifle dangled in his hands. At the edge of his vision he saw Élise lob a grenade over the barricade, in case the Germans were regrouping. The explosion made the ground and the barrier tremble, but Thibaut did not move.

The Vélo tipped forward, back onto both wheels. She accelerated toward him but he made himself stay still. She bore down and her wheels were a burr. Adrenaline took him with the certainty of impact, until on a final instant too quick to see she tilted and passed instead so close to him that Thibaut's clothes were tugged in the rush of her air.

Tires singing, the cycle-presence wove between the shattered buildings of the Cité de Trévise, into ruins and shadows, out of sight.

Thibaut at last exhaled. When he could control his shaking, he turned to the passenger. He went to where she lay.

The woman was dying. She had been hammered by the German fire the Vélo had ignored. Some fleeting influence at that powerful intersection of streets meant all the holes in her flesh were dry and puckered, but blood spilled from her mouth as if insisting on one outlet. She coughed and tried to speak.

"Did you see?" Élise was shouting. Thibaut knelt and put his hand on the fallen woman's forehead. The partisans gathered. "She was *riding the Vélo!*" Élise said. "What does that *mean*? How in hell did she *control* it?"

"Not well," said Virginie.

The passenger's dark dress was dirty and ripped. Her scarf spread out on the road and framed her face. She furrowed her brow as if thoughtful. As if considering a problem. She was not much older than Thibaut, he thought. She looked at him with urgent eyes.

"It's . . . it's . . ." she said.

"I think that's English," he said quietly.

Cédric stepped forward and tried to murmur prayers and Virginie shoved him sharply away.

The dying woman took Thibaut's hand. "Here," she whispered. "He came. Wolf. Gang." She gasped out little bursts. Thibaut put his ear close to her mouth. "Gerhard," she said. "The doctor. The priest."

She was not looking at him any more, Thibaut realized, but past him, behind him. His skin itched in Paris's attention. He turned.

Behind the windows of the nearest building, overlooking them, a slowly shifting universe of fetal globs and scratches unfolded. A morass of dark colors, vivid on a blacker dark. The shapes rattled. They tapped the glass. A manif storm had come from within the house to witness this woman's death.

As everyone gathered watched the black virtue behind the windows, Thibaut felt the woman's fingers on his own. He gripped hers in turn. But she did not want a moment's last solicitude. She pried his hand open. She put something in it. Thibaut felt and knew instantly that it was a playing card.

When he turned back to her the woman was dead.

Thibaut was loyal Main à plume. He could not have said why he slipped the card into his pocket without letting his comrades see.

On the stones under the woman's other hand she had written letters on the road with her index finger as a nib. Her nail was wet with black ink from somewhere, provided by the city in that final moment of her need. She had written two last words.

FALL ROT.

———

Now it's months later, and Thibaut huddles in a Paris doorway, his hand in his pocket to hold that card again. Over his own clothes he wears a woman's blue-and-gold pajamas.

The sky is screaming. Two Messerschmitts come in below the clouds, chased by Hurricanes. Slates explode under British fire and the planes tear out of their dives. One of the German aircraft coils suddenly back in a virtuoso maneuver with weapons blazing and in a burning gust an RAF plane unfolds in the air, opening like hands, like a blown kiss, fire descending, turning an unseen house below to dust.

The other Messerschmitt veers toward the Seine. The roofs shake again, this time from below.

Something comes up from inside Paris.

A pale tree-wide tendril, shaggy with bright foliage. It rises. Clutches of buds or fruit the size of human heads quiver. It blooms vastly above the skyline.

The German pilot flies straight at the vivid flowers, as if smitten, plant-drunk. He plunges for the vegetation. It spreads trembling leaves. The great vine whips up one last house-height and takes the plane in its coils. It yanks it down below the roofs, into the streets, out of sight.

There is no explosion. The snagged aircraft is just gone, into the deeps of the city.

The other planes frantically disperse. Thibaut waits while they go. He lets his heart slow. When he sets his face and steps out at last it is under a clean sky.

Thibaut is twenty-four, hard and thin and strong. His eyes move constantly as he keeps watch in all directions: he has the fretful aggression and the gritted teeth of the new Parisian. He keeps his hair and his nails short. He squints with more than just suspicion: he does not have the spectacles he suspects he might need. Beneath his bright woman's nightclothes he wears a dirty darned white shirt, dark trousers and suspenders, worn black boots. It has been some days since Thibaut has shaved. He's scabbed and stinking.

Those pilots were foolhardy. Paris's air is full of reasons not to fly.

There are worse things than garden airplane traps like the one that took the Messerschmitt. The chimneys of Paris are buffeted by ecstatic avian storm clouds. Bones inflated like airships. Flocks of bat-winged businessmen and ladies in outdated coats shout endless monologues of special offers and clog planes' propellers with their own questionable meat. Thibaut has watched mono- and bi- and triplane geometries, winged spheres and huge ghastly spindles, a long black-curtained window, all flying like animate dead over the tops of houses, pursuing an errant Heinkel Greif bomber, to negate it with an unliving touch.

Thibaut can mostly name the manifestations he sees, when they have names.

Before the war he had already committed to the movement which spawned them, which detractors had derided as passé, as powerless. "I don't care about fashion!" is what he had told his amused mother, waving the publications he bought, sight-unseen, from a sympathetic bookseller in rue Ruelle, who knew to put aside for him anything affiliated. "This is about liberation!" The dealer, Thibaut would come to realize, long after those days, would sometimes accept paltry payment from his enthusiastic and ignorant young customer, in exchange for rarities. The last package he sent reached Thibaut's home two days before he left it for the last time.

When later he had watched the Germans march into the city, the sight of their columns by the Arc de Triomphe had looked to Thibaut like a grim collage, an agitprop warning.

Now he walks wide deserted streets of the sixteenth, a long way from his own arenas, his rifle raised and the gold trim of his skirts flapping. The sun bleaches the ruins. A miraculously uneaten cat races out from under a burnt-out German tank to find another hole.

Weeds grow through old cars and the floors of newspaper kiosks. They cosset the skeletons of the fallen. Huge sunflowers root all over, and the grass underfoot is speck-led with plants that did not exist until the blast: plants that make noise; plants that move. Lovers' flowers, their petals elliptical eyes and throbbing cartoon hearts bunched alternately in the mouths of up-thrust snakes that are their stems, that sway and stare as Thibaut warily passes.

Rubble and greenery fall away and the sky opens as he reaches the river. Thibaut watches for monsters.

In the shallows and the mud of the Île aux Cygnes, human hands crawl under spiral shells. A congregation of Seine sharks thrash up dirty froth below the Pont de Gren-elle. Rolling and rising, they eye him as he approaches and bite at the bobbing corpse of a horse. In front of each dorsal fin, each shark is hollow-backed, with a canoe seat.

Thibaut walks the bridge above them. Midway across he stops. He stands in plain sight. His soldier's nerves itch for cover but he makes himself stand and look. He surveys the altered city.

Jags of ruin, a fallen outline. Framed against the flat bright sky to the north-east, the Eiffel Tower looms. The tower's steepling top half dangles where it has always been, where the Pont d'Iéna meets the Quai Branly, above ordered gardens, but halfway to the earth the metal ends. There's nothing tethering it to the ground. It hangs, trun-cated. A flock of the brave remaining birds of Paris swoop below the stumps of its struts, forty storeys up. The half-tower points with a long shadow.

Where are the cells of Main à plume now? How many have succumbed?

Months back, after the Vélo, Thibaut had been, you could perhaps say, called to action, insofar as anyone could be called to anything any more. An invitation reached him by the city's networks. Word from old comrades.

"They told me you run things here," the young scout had said. Thibaut did not like that. "Will you come?"

Thibaut remembers how heavy the card had been then in his pocket. Did someone know he had it? Was that for what they were calling?

On the card is a stylized pale woman. She stares twice in rotational symmetry. Her yellow hair becomes two big cats that swaddle her. Below each of her faces is a blue, profile, closed-eyed other, unless they, too, are her. There is a black keyhole in the top right corner and the bottom left.

"Come on," Thibaut had said to the messenger. "Why do they want me? I'm protecting the ninth."

A while after he declined came word of a dramatic sortie, one that failed in a terrible way. Rumors of who had died: a roll-call of his teachers.

Goodbye, he thinks at last, all these weeks later. His nightclothes snap in the wind.

━━

Thibaut was fifteen when the S-Blast came.

A call like a far-off siren, by the river, and a wave of shadow and silence racing out and leaving young Thibaut wheezing for breath and blinking with eyes gone momentarily unseeing, and the city poised and primed behind it, something emergent, something irrupting into and from its unconscious. A dream invaded from below. What had been the world's prettiest city was now populated by its own unpretty imaginings, and by the ugliness of the pit.

Thibaut was not a natural guerilla, but, hating the invader and struggling not to die, he had learned to fight. Parisian, he had been sucked into an apocalypse; to which, he would quickly come to learn, to his conflicted shock, he was affiliated.

Those first days had been all made of madness, assaults by impossible figures and misremembered bones. Streetfighting Nazis and Resistance had killed each other in panic as they tried to contain reveries of which they could not make sense. On the second night after the blast, terrified Wehrmacht, trying to secure a zone, had shepherded Thibaut and his family and all their neighbors into a barbed-wire pen in the street. There they shuffled, clutching bags containing whatever they had managed to grab, while the soldiers yelled abuse and argued with each other.

There had come a massive howl, getting quickly closer. Already by then Thibaut recognized the voice of something manifested.

Everyone screamed at the sound. A panicking officer

waved his weapon, aimed it at last, decisively, at the gathered civilians. He fired.

Some soldiers tried and failed to stop him doing it again, others joined in with him. Over the echoes of carnage the manif kept up its cry. Thibaut remembers how his father fell, and his mother, trying as she did to shield him, and how he fell himself after them, not knowing if his legs had given way or if he was playing dead to live. He had heard more shouts and the manif voice closer still and the sounds of new violence.

And then finally when all the screaming and the shots were done, Thibaut raised his head slowly from amid the dead, like a seal from the sea.

He was looking into a metal grille. The visor of a plumed knight's helmet. It was vastly too big. It was centimeters from his own face.

The helmeted presence stared at him. He blinked and its metal trembled. He and it were all that moved. All the Germans were dead or gone. The manif lurched but Thibaut was still. He waited for it to kill him and it held his gaze and let him be. It was the first of many manifs to do so.

The thing swayed up and back from the flesh and debris of the killing ground. It reared, seven, eight meters tall, an impossible composite of tower and human and a great shield, all out of scale and made one looming body, handless arms held almost dainty by its sides, its left thronging with horseflies. It declared itself mournfully, an echoing call of faceplate hinges. When that noise ebbed the huge thing stalked away at last on three limbs: one huge spurred man's leg; a pair of women's high-heeled feet.

And there was quiet. And Thibaut, war's boy, had crawled shivering at last through the hecatomb in a field of rubble, to where he found the corpses of his parents and wept.

He has often imagined a vengeful hunt for that officer who first fired, but Thibaut cannot remember what he looked like. Or for the man or men whose ammunition killed his parents, but he doesn't know who they were. They were all probably among those shot by their own comrades in the chaos, in any case, or crushed by bricks when the manif toppled the façade.

━━━

In rue Giroux, masonry slumps in sloppy drifts. Bricks bounce down a broken slope and a young woman emerges, her face bloody and filthy and her hair spiked with dirt. She does not see Thibaut. He watches her bite her nails and scurry on.

One of the trapped thousands. The Nazis will never allow Paris to contaminate France. All roads in and out are locked down.

When it was clear that the manifs, the new things with their new powers, would not disappear, before the Reich had settled for this containment, it had tried first to destroy, then to use them. Or to bring forth its own, less

capricious than its infernal allies. The Nazis had even
succeeded in invoking a few things with their manifology:
incompetent statuettes; a Céline *weltgeist,* fungal lassi-
tude, semi-sentient dirt and enervation infecting house
after house. But their successes were few, unsustainable,
uncommandable.

Now, years on, it seems to Thibaut that the number of
manifs has started to diminish. That this is the second
epoch of the post-blast city.

Of course Paris still teems. *Just walk if you doubt that,*
he thinks, *see what you meet.* Enigmarelle, foppish robot
staggered out of an exhibition guide, arms out to lethally
embrace. The dreaming cat, as big as a child and incompetently bipedal, watching with sentient intent. *You will
encounter such figures,* Thibaut thinks. *For a while yet.*

And if you go on walking like that and stay safe and
keep out of sight then you will come some time to be alone
again and there will be a stretch of window and bricks
untouched by war and you could, for an instant, believe
yourself back in old Paris.

I miss nothing, Thibaut insists to himself once more.
Not the pre-war days, nor the recent relative safety of the
ninth arrondissement. The stranded Nazis in the tenth
could never take those streets, or the altered landscapes
they crisscrossed, the sagelands, smoothed alpine topographies like sagging drapes, houses of frozen rooms full of
clocks, places where the geography echoed itself. The

ninth was too completely made of recalcitrant art for anyone to take. It would shelter no one but the partisans of
that art—the Surrealist stay-behinds, soldiers of the unconscious. Main à plume.

I don't miss a thing. Thibaut clenches his fist on his
weapon.

Each riverbank tree here is in a different season. Dead
leaves and live. Thibaut wants railway lines. Routes out.
Under one lamppost, it is night. He leans against it and
sits and for long minutes looks up at stars.

Do I even deserve these places any more? They came at
the wrong time and they came in the wrong way. Liberation was fucked up. But if Thibaut can find *no* spark of
joy in them, he thinks, maybe he is no better than one of
Stalin's men. Or a drone for de Gaulle, an enemy of true
freedom.

That isn't me, he thinks. *No.*

He stands and steps back into the sunlight beyond the
tiny manif nightlet, and as he does a howl fills the street.

Instantly Thibaut drops, takes cover behind the stub of
a pillar, weapon raised. War has taught him how to be
very still. That is not a human noise—nor, he is sure, that
of a manif.

He waits. He controls his breathing and listens to a
heavy approach. Something comes slowly into view.
Thibaut sights down his rifle and tightens his grip.

A swaying body like a great bull's. Its flanks are

bloodied, and rainbowed as if with petrol on water. On its brow the thing has many long, gray, random horns, some broken. It bellows again and shows meat-eater tusks.

It does not move with the dreamlike specificity of a manif but with a thudding, broken step that he can feel through the ground. It comes with nothing of that stir of recognition—even at something inconceivable that he has never previously seen—that a manif brings him. It oozes and drips and raises nausea in Thibaut. Its blood crackles and smokes and hits the pavement in spots of flame. The beast shakes its head and flecks fly from its horns to land wetly. Thibaut's innards spasm, and he knows from that clench that those are gobbets of manif.

If the devils and the living art cannot avoid each other, they will fight, terribly. The artflesh dripping from the demon's face is fresh.

In the days after the S-Blast, the German forces and the newcomer manifs had been joined, appallingly, by such as this misplaced invader, battalions from below.

The exigencies of survival sent some of Thibaut's comrades trying to make sense of these fallen, now risen, embarrassments. They accumulated expertise from bad books they hunted and found. They cajoled information from captured German summoners and specialist priests in Alesch's nascent bishopric. The intrepid eavesdropped on snips of the demons' bayed discussions, they pieced together information, parsed rumors of ill-tempered pacts between Hell and the Reich. Élise might have been able to tell him what kind of fiend it is he looks at, as he prays, if to no God, that it will not look at him: all Thibaut knows is that it is a devil, and a big one.

Like most of its kind the thing is obviously in pain. But that size, whatever its injuries or sickness, they will not help him. The few trinkets he has in his pack for use against the infernal are inadequate: it will kill him if it finds him.

But the beast shambles painfully away on what seems a varying number of legs and does not look in his direction. It leaves a trail of burning blood and broken ground.

He waits until it turns off the street, out of sight, and he listens to it haul itself away, and he waits longer until he can hear nothing. Only then does Thibaut slump at last, fingering his nightskirt. Even that, he thinks, tracing the edge of its hem, would not have saved him. *I should get off the streets,* he thinks. Then: *Maybe I should take the Métro,* he taunts himself.

Thibaut considers his dead, in the forest. He considers the ruined plan, the assault from which he exiled himself.

From his bag he pulls out a pencil and a stained old schoolbook, folded many times. He opens his war note-books.

I'm not a fucking deserter. The mission is vacant. I'm not a deserter.

Thibaut was nearly seventeen when, following survivors' stories and the noise of shots and burnt and uncannily twisted remains of German patrols and the intuitions that sometimes beset him, he tracked down the Main à plume in the ruins.

He was waving scrappy publications at them as he came, trembling so hard with nerves that he made the selectors who met him and ushered him into their compound laugh, not unkindly.

"This is you, isn't it?" he kept saying, pointing at the pages, the names. They kept laughing when he told them, "I want to join you."

They tested him. When he said he couldn't shoot—he'd not yet held a gun—they joked that he'd have to try automatic shooting. Like automatic writing, they said. "You know who it was said the simplest act of Surrealism is to fire randomly into a crowd?" He did, and they liked that.

Other examinations. They pointed at certain objects from the junk that filled their cellar, asking him if they were surreal or just trash. Thibaut looked at the configurations and muttered answers too quickly for thought—a claw-and-ball chair leg was nothing, an empty cigar box and a hairbrush were surreal, so on. He corrected himself only once, over what he could never later remember. They looked at him more thoughtfully when he was done.

When one of the questioners took off his shoe to rub his

toe, with boldness not yet characteristic Thibaut took it from the surprised man, picked up a candlestick he had previously dismissed as mere object and placed it inside the old leather. "Now it's surreal," he said. The glances of the selectors—artists, clerks, and curators turned guerilla—had not escaped him.

"You want to fight, I understand," the half-shod man said, looking at him sideways. "Right now, though . . . with all this . . . why like *this*? Why with us? With the city like this, don't we have greater needs than poetry?"

Immediately Thibaut almost shouted a response. " 'We refuse to flee poetry for reality,' " he said. " 'But we refuse to flee reality for poetry.' " The men and women blinked at him. " 'No one should say our actions are superfluous,' " Thibaut recited. " 'If they do, we'll say *the superfluous supposes the necessary*.' "

He had recognized the question, the last test. It, and his answer, were the words of Jean-François Chabrun, speaking for the *franc-tireurs*, Surrealist irregulars, left in Paris when the Nazis came. A prophecy, a promise written after one cataclysm and just before another. They had carried it over after that next, the S-Blast, and Thibaut granted it fidelity.

He will never be a sharpshooter. He is an adequate hand-to-hand fighter at best. Thibaut was admitted to the Main à plume because of his way of seeing, the connections he makes, the synchronicity he notes and invokes.

They taught him to conduct what they called *disponibil-ité*, to be a receiver. To tap objective chance.

In rooms at the top of leaning houses, in a city become free-fire zone and hunting grounds for the impossible, Thibaut learned survival and poetry, from Régine Rau-fast, Edouard Jaguer, Rius, Dotremont, Chabrun himself, techniques he would take with him later, when training was done, full of thanks and solidarity, to spread the resis-tance, to join with others, and recruit. In his company, Jacques Hérold set a black chain on fire.

In the post-blast miasma, all Parisians grew invisible organs that flex in the presence of the marvelous. Thibaut's are strong.

The Surrealists trapped behind had known immedi-ately what the newly appeared figures were that the explo-sion had brought. Not the devils, those tawdry bugbears: them they considered as little as they could. But the *oth-ers,* they knew. They were the first to recognize them, to try to develop a strategy for life and for urban war that afforded them respect. The Main à plume owed them, not obedience, but a kind of fealty: this was hardly the hoped-for insurrection, but these *were* Surrealist glimmers, these manifs. They were convulsively beautiful, and they were arrived. The poets and artists and philosophers, resistance activists, secret scouts and troublemakers, had become, as they must, soldiers.

Now, alone, Thibaut drinks to the freedom of Paris

from a standpipe in a square full of bricks like failed flowers.

———

Months ago, his scouts in the ninth reported demons in a charnel-house off Clichy. Thibaut and the comrades of his cell had looked at each other in horror.

"They're not with Nazi handlers," Virginie said. She was a recent recruit to the Surrealist resistance, ferocious but young and ignorant. "They're feral. How urgent is it? Do we have to . . . ?"

"You've not dealt with them before," Thibaut said. "Or you'd know."

The thing was, he told her, you could no more accommodate devils than you could a splinter gone septic, an allergic reaction. The power of the arrondissement had kept them out, so far, but for occasional lumbering, blundering intruders. But now they had established themselves, if they were not driven out or destroyed, they would transform the ninth into a zone of blood and infernal agony. The Surrealists had to prepare an exorcism.

There was a pleasure in some of the process and accoutrements, relics of wizardry that had embarrassed the Enlightenment. Other necessities, though, stank of clericalism, and the partisans were disgusted that they were efficacious. It was with distaste that Thibaut and Élise took a bag of crucifixes, bottles of holy water, bells, to Father Cédric. Élise made a joke—she, the rabbi's grand-daughter, carrying such things. The old priest performed desultory benedictions and they paid him in cigarettes and food.

"Turn the other cheek, Father," said Élise at his expression. "Find some Free French if you want willing sheep to patronize. Until then, this is a marriage of inconvenience. You want to walk? There's the door."

He was safer in their company, and they in his. An uncomfortable symbiosis. The Surrealists despised his calling, and he them for their militant atheism, but everyone knew it helped to have a priest perform certain absurdities of his trade if it was demons you had to fight.

"Why?" Thibaut asked Élise when they left again. "Why do you think it does work? It's not as if any of this stuff is *true*."

"Maybe devils love ritual as much as people do," she said.

However they might mock and bully him, Thibaut's crew had a degree of unfriendly respect for Cédric: whatever else the man was, he was Resistance. In these streets, his very tradition had become unlikely dissent. Unlike so many clergy, he had refused to make any peace at all with the new Church of Paris, or with its leader, Robert Alesch.

For months before the reconfiguration, the Abbé Alesch

had been a well-known preacher against the Nazis. A very few intimates had known, too, that he worked as part of Jeannine Picabia's clandestine network, réseau Gloria. He'd been courier and confidant, able, as a priest, to pass through the zones, carrying messages and contraband. His Gloria comrades called him "Bishop," and he heard their confessions.

He was a double-agent. In the S-Blast's aftermath, he had sold his comrades to his Nazi paymasters, and almost every one of them had died. Alesch, V-man, informer, paid not thirty pieces of silver but twelve thousand francs a month.

Two austere activists, Suzanne Dechevaux-Dumesnil and her lover, the Irishman Beckett, had escaped from the carnage of Gloria. They had gotten word out of Alesch's perfidy, but he had not cowered. Rather, he had inaugurated a theology of betrayal. A Catholicism of collaboration— with the German invaders, and with those invaders from below. Rome denounced him, and he denounced Rome back. He made himself Bishop in his own Führer-funded church.

On their hatred for Alesch, Cédric and the Surrealists could agree.

At twilight the fighters had ascended to the roofscape, their guns loaded with that sardonically blessed ammunition.

In Paris you had to be ready to fight art *and* the Hellish—
not to mention Nazis—so they labored under weapons for
all eventualities.

Thibaut was ready for manifs. He had his expertise, he
could perform cathexis, or use a weapon itself manifested
against them.

Humans, of course, could be killed with almost anything.

The partisans picked like wood-gatherers through
copses of chimneys. Among the old bricks, dead crows,
slates, and gutters, Thibaut saw pendulums and figures
made of string. The detritus of the surreal, evanescent
unconsciousnesses. There were doors at roofs' edges. Dim
things walking too close, at which he would not look.

Then the faint sound of screaming. They approached
warily. With the sky huge around them, the Main à
plume reached the source of noise. They stared down into
a warehouse's cracked skylight as if it were a scrying
pool.

Far below, a man in robes spasmed suspended in the
air above the chamber's dusty floor. He thrashed amid
monsters.

A trumpet-nosed beast with fish eyes swung a cudgel in
brutal percussion. A legless thing with bat wings thrashed
him with its spiked and suckered tail. Rag doll animals
chewed the man's fingers and gouged him with their horns.

"My God," Virginie whispered. "Come on." The
resistance fighters grit their teeth in disgust and quickly

readied weapons. A lizard-like doll-thing snarled, a hairy pig-faced assailant leered between assaults.

"Wait," Thibaut managed to say. He held up his hand. "Look. Look at his clothes."

"Get out of the way, Thib," said Pierre, aiming through the glass.

"*Wait*. He moved just like that a moment ago," Thibaut said. The man screamed again. "*Listen.*" Moments passed, and the distinct wavering cry repeated. "Look at the devils," Thibaut said. "Look at *him*."

The floating man's eyes were unfocused and as flat as concrete. There was a precision to his sand-colored robes, his beard. He wailed and writhed and his cries grew neither louder nor quieter and the blood pattered unendingly beneath him in a pool that did not spread.

"Those demons," Thibaut said at last, "are too healthy. They're repeating like a scratched record. They aren't demons. And what they're torturing isn't a man."

The changing streets of Paris echoed now with the slamming of Hell-hard feet. They had burst from sewers after the blast came, torn open trees like broken doors, hurtling out into the world as the manifs did, though they were not like them, nothing like them, though the explosion had palpably been not of their nature. As if the explosion was not their birth but their excuse. They swam up into the light through pavements made lava, roaring up from a glimpsed painscape. Giants with cobwebs for faces, crab-headed generals encased in teeth. And so on. They wore armor and gold. They cast pestilential spells and yammered with abyssal gusto.

But the demons winced through their sneers. They rubbed their skins gingerly when they thought they weren't observed. When they killed and tormented it was in faintly needy fashion. They seemed anxious. They stank not only of sulfur but infection. Sometimes they wept with pain.

The devils of Paris would not shut up. They declaimed as they came, in a hundred languages, they hissed and howled descriptions of their hadal cities, and beat their claws on the sigils they wore, of the houses of the pit, and they shouted rather too often to those they hunted and killed that it was from *Hell* that they came, and so that everyone should be terrified.

They had come flank-by-side onto the streets with Nazis and their Vichy allies, patrolling with specialist witch-officers, launching joint attacks, with bullets and bombs and the spit and boiling blood of Hell. It was clear: whereas the manifs had no overseers, the Reich had *invoked* these other things to win the war. Their collaboration was not always successful. There were times when, even during onslaughts against their enemies, their bickering exploded into bad-tempered massacres, fiends and Nazis ripping each other open while their targets, their own slaughter interrupted, listened bemused to screaming accusations on both sides.

Now they were here, to those who watched closely the devils were as cowed as their army handlers, as stranded in impossible Paris as everyone else. They came up but were not seen descending. Hide outside their lairs—as did the bravest or suicidal human spies—and you might sometimes hear them sobbing for a Gehenna from which by incompetent demonology it seemed they were permanently exiled.

You could learn to see that the living art of the city intimidated them. It sent them scurrying if outnumbered, or nervously on the attack if not.

"Those," Thibaut said to his comrades that night on the roof, of the devil-like things below them, "are not demons. They're manifs."

Living images. *Images* of demons, and of their victim. And not even sentient like most of the art come alive in New Paris, but looping.

"No!" said Pierre, bringing his rifle back up. "Fucking bullshit," he said, and aimed again. But he did not fire, and his comrades watched the scene repeat, until Élise gently pushed his gun down.

━━

Thibaut whispers to those gone.

It's night but he keeps walking. He wants cool air and dark to draw its edges into white Paris stone like drafting ink. So he walks crumbling streets until the moon arrives, then closes his eyes and walks more, lets his unconscious pull him toward whichever moldering house it will, feeling for safety. *I'll sleep an hour,* he thinks. *Two, three hours, that's all.*

When his fingers touch wood he looks again. He forces the door. His footsteps squelch on a swampy carpet. He walks with his gun up.

From a mantelpiece of a large front room a dream mammal watches him with marmoset eyes. It cringes at him. Blood drips from sickle claws. In the puddles on the floor, a drowned woman lies facedown. Thibaut sees her mottled shoulder blades: he abruptly knows, with an inner flex of insight, that the animal is waiting for her to rot.

He should be quiet at night—especially on this, his last night—but he is full of the rage of a failed soldier. He aims at the carnivore bush-baby.

It hesitates, as manifs do before him. Thibaut surrenders his will and fires, Surrealist-style.

His bullets sway. They correct mid-flight, burst into the thing as it leaps, slam it against the wall where it thumps its limbs and dissolves like tar.

Thibaut waits. His weapon smokes. Nothing appears. He goes to turn the dead woman but stops, holds his face in his hands and wonders if he will cry. He cannot sleep now.

Two days after the Main à plume's abortive assault on the non-demons, as Thibaut ate his stale-bread breakfast, Virginie put a book on the table in front of him.

"What's this?" he said.

She flipped through engravings to a picture of a trumpeting thing, a spiked tail, a horde of little devils. He recognized them. They beset the same St. Anthony that they had seen a few streets away.

"It's by Schongauer," she said.

"Where did you get this?"

"A library."

Thibaut shook his head at her foolishness or bravery. To plunder a library! Books were not safe.

"Thing is," she said. "That manif? Of this image? I don't think it just self-generated. It's not close enough. To the heart of the S-Blast."

In the fecund shock waves of the explosion, it was not only the Surrealists' own dreams that had manifested. Born with them were figures from Symbolism and Decadence, imaginings of the Surrealists' ancestors and beloveds, ghosts from their proto-canon. Now Redon's leering ten-legged spider hunted at one end of rue Jean Lantier, chattering its big teeth. A figure with Arcimboldo's coagulate fruit face stalked the boundaries of the Saint-Ouen market.

"If this was Dürer, maybe," she said, "or Piranesi. Schongauer? He's important, but I don't think he's core

enough to manifest spontaneously. I think someone invoked this deliberately."

"Who?" Thibaut said. "Why?"

"The Nazis. Maybe they want devils that'll follow orders better. I think they want their own manifs," Virginie
said. "I think they're still trying." They regarded each other.
Pictured their enemies tugging at images from pages with
whatever invocatory engines they could put together. "The
Führer himself," Virginie said heavily, "is an *artist,* after
all." Reproductions of his barely competent watercolors,
his hesitant lines, his featureless faces, his vacuous, pretty,
empty urban façades, had circulated as curios in occult
Paris. Virginie and Thibaut shared a glance of contempt.

━━

Whatever their source, those devil-manifs were weak,
without even the verve to fully emerge. *They're probably
there still,* thinks Thibaut. Endlessly eating endless, dumb,
saintly prey.

He approaches Garibaldi and boulevard Pasteur. Behind shutters he makes out the guttering of candles. These
houses are tiny communes. A family in each room, stoves
burning broken chairs, routes holed between walls. House-
villages. Thibaut falls asleep and dreams as he trudges
Haussmann's boulevards.

He dreams Élise falling toward him in blood that ob-
scures her face. He sees Virginie, and Paul, and Jean, and

the rest of them, and he is too late to do anything but cradle their dying heads in the dark of the forest.

Thibaut does not cry out but he does jolt himself awake, still walking. He sets his face back into a city sneer.

At a junction, shining in the moon's white light, there is motion, and Thibaut slows. Two skeletons. They jerk their fleshless limbs. They walk a slow circle.

Thibaut is still. The dead feet click.

Alain, the best officer his cell ever voted into place, would treat such prim Delvaux bones, or the dens of fossils, prone Mallo skeletons shaking themselves repeatedly apart, with great respect. It had not stopped three of them jabbing him to death one humming hot June day with their own splintering matter.

Thibaut backs away. He does not want to fight manifs.

The organ in him, his new muscle, cramps at a sudden spasm of manif energy. It comes from somewhere *else*. He staggers. It comes again, so hard he doubles up.

There is a rapid cracking of shots. The skeletons do not pause. The sounds are to the north. They are away from Thibaut's route, but close, and his own insides still grip him from within, tug him, and when he runs, it is, almost to his own bewilderment, toward the firing.

Through a boundary into the seventh. His ears pop. Another shot. Thibaut smells sap.

The avenue de Breteuil is full of aspen trees. Their boughs stretch out to touch the houses. The complex of Les Invalides, that sprawling and once-opulent old military zone, is out of sight, has been overcome by millennial vegetation. Lampposts struggle up from roots and roofs from the canopy. The Cathedral of Saint-Louis des Invalides is filled with bark. The Musée de l'Armée is being emptied, with slow, vegetable disorder, its weapons gripped and tugged over weeks out of their cases by curious undergrowth.

Another shot: a flock of night things disperses. Something laughs. A woman runs out of the forest. She wears thick glasses, tweed trousers, and jacket, all smeared with woodland muck. She labors under bags and equipment, waves a pistol.

There are growls, the snarl of breath. Beasts come rushing through the trees after her, with strange quick staggering.

They are little tables, stiff board bodies, unbending wooden legs, thrashing tails, and ferocious canine faces. They scream and bite the air. Fanged furniture jerking across the rough ground.

Thibaut hisses and steps past the stumbling woman into her pursuers' path, between them and their quarry. They'll veer from him, he thinks, as most manifs do.

But they attack. They keep coming.

He is almost too slow, in his shock, to bring up his gun.

He fires as the first animal thing leaps, sends the growling table flying in an explosion of splinters.

Others hurl themselves at him, and his cotton night-clothes are suddenly as tough as metal. He swings his arms. The pajamas grip Thibaut, make him an instrument, propel him fast and hard. A wood-and-taxidermy predator reaches him, biting, and Thibaut's clothed arm comes down and snaps its spine.

He stands between the woman and the wolf-tables, snarling as bestially as the pack. The tables inch forward. With a burst of creative chance Thibaut shoots the closest right in its snarl and sends it down in blood and sawdust.

There's shouting from the forest. He can see two, three figures in the trees. SS uniforms. A man in a dark coat, calling in German. *Quick! Be careful! The dogs—*

A burly officer fires right at him out of the shadows. Thibaut howls. But the shots ricochet from his chest. The soldier frowns as Thibaut brings his own rickety old rifle up and shoots and misses of course and reloads while the man still watches, stupid and slow, and Thibaut fires again, this time with *disponibilité,* and puts him down.

Wolf-tables bite. A Nazi cracks a whip, to *rally* them, to gather them, and Thibaut snatches as the leather swings. It slaps and wraps his hand and makes it numb but he grips. By him the woman drops, pushes her fingers into the topsoil: the furniture that menaces her twitches and backs away. Thibaut yanks the whip-holder toward him by his weapon and punches him back again, sending him flying into the dark.

The Germans hesitate. The pack howls. Thibaut smacks a tree hard enough to make it quake, showing his pajama-ed strength. The attackers retreat, into the forest, back out of sight, toward the corridors of Les Invalides. The humans call as they run, and the little tables follow the sound, baring their teeth as the darkness takes them.

"Thank you," the woman says. "Thank you." She is gathering her fallen things. "Come on." She speaks French with an American accent, a thin and cultured voice.

"What in hell was that?" Thibaut says. The man he just hit is dead. Thibaut goes through his pockets. "I've never seen *anything* like those things before."

"They're called wolf-tables," the woman says. "Manifest from an imagining by a man called Brauner. We must go."

Thibaut stares at her. Eventually he says, "Brauner's have fox parts. Those tables were bigger than any I've seen, and their fur was more gray. They didn't look like foxes. It's as if they were crossbred. The soldiers called them 'dogs.' And they were *doing what they were told.* And . . ." He looks away from her. "As I say, I've never seen any manifs, including wolf-tables, like them before." *And they came right at* me. *They didn't hesitate.*

After a moment the woman says, "Please excuse me. Of course. I misunderstood."

"Wolf-tables are scavengers," Thibaut goes on. "One shot should have dispersed them." They gorge themselves, trying to fill stomachs they don't have, clogging up their throats till they vomit blood and meat and spit and then eating helplessly again. "Wolf-tables aren't brave."

"Of *course* you know manifs," the woman says. "I apologize. I didn't mean to be rude. But please . . . We have to go."

"Who are you?"

She is a few years older than he. Her face is round with high flushed cheeks, her hair is dark and short. She looks at him from where she stoops among the roots.

"What are you doing here?" Thibaut says, and then instantly thinks he knows.

"I'm Sam," she says. He takes her satchel. "Hey," she says.

He upends the bag.

"What are you *doing*?" she shouts.

He scatters a camera, canisters of film, several battered books. The camera is not old. He feels no manif charge. These are not surreal objects. He stares at them. He was expecting scavenger spoils. He was expecting old gloves; a stuffed snake; things that are dusty; a wineglass half melted in lava and embedded in stone; bits of a typewriter; a barnacled book that has rested underwater; tweezers that change what they touch.

Thibaut had thought this woman a battle junkie, a magpie of war. Artifact hunters creep past the barricades to seek, extract, and sell stuff born or altered by the blast. Batteries of odd energies. Objects foraged out of the Nazis' quarantine, fenced for colossal sums in the black markets of the world outside. Manifs stolen while the partisans fight for liberation, while Thibaut and his comrades face down devils and fascists and errant art, and die.

He almost has more respect for his enemies than for the dealers in such goods. In the satchel Thibaut expected to find a spoon covered with fur; a candle; a pebble in a box. He blinks. He folds and unfolds the Nazi's whip.

Sam checks the camera for damage. "What was that for?" she says.

Thibaut prods the books with his toe as though they might turn into more expected spoils. She smacks his foot away. Maps of Paris. Journals: *Minotaure; Documents; Le Surréalisme au service de la révolution; La Révolution surréaliste; View*.

"Why do you have these?" he says. His voice is hushed.

The woman brushes the covers clean. "You thought I was a treasure-hunter. Jesus." She looks at him through her camera's viewfinder and he puts his hand in front of his face. She presses the button and it clicks and he feels something in his blood. He keeps staring at her journals, thinking of those he once carried. He left them, years ago, when he took his leave of training. An odd homage to his instructors, those spare copies, pages full of their own work.

The woman sighs with relief. "If you'd broken *this,* you and I would've been on a bad footing."

She puts the camera strap around her neck and brushes dirt from a big leather notebook. She offers her hand.

"I'm not here to steal," she says. "I'm here to keep a record."

———

After he left his dead parents behind him, before he found those who would become his comrades, Thibaut, not yet sixteen, had hid and crept and wandered for a long time. When he reached the edge of the old city, he had secreted himself where he could see gangs of terrified, trapped citizens run, launch themselves at barricades thrown up at the perimeter of the blasted zone, from beyond which the Nazi guards fired remorseless fusillades, killing them until they understood there was no way to leave. In those first days some German soldiers, too, had run at their compatriots' positions, waving and shouting to be let across the street and out. If they came too close, they, too, were put down. Those officers and men who saw and hung back, pleading, were commanded over loudspeakers to remain within the affected radius, to await instructions.

He retreated to the unsafety of Paris. There Thibaut

slept where he could and hunted for food and wiped his eyes and hid from terrible things. He crept repeatedly back to those outskirts, though, tried to scout a way out, again and again, failed every time. The city was rigorously sealed.

At last one night under pounding rain, sheltering in the ruins of a tobacconist and leafing listlessly through his belongings, he found in his pack that last stack of pamphlets and books he had received, the day the blast had blasted. Thibaut cut the string that still bound it.

Géographie nocturne, a pamphlet of poems. A review; *La Main à plume*. The Surrealism of those still in the occupied city. Written in resistance, under occupation. He had seen the names Chabrun, Patin, Dotrement. The rain cracked the window onto nocturnal geography.

"'Those who are asleep,'" Thibaut had read, "'are workers and collaborators in what goes on in the universe.'"

He opened the second volume onto Chabrun's "État de présence." That defense of poetry, antifascist rage. The statement of intent of these stay-behind faithful, that, much later, Thibaut would recite to the Main à plume selectors, to pass his entry test. A Surrealist state of presence. He riffled the pages and the first words he read were almost the document's last.

"Should we go? Stay? If you can stay, stay . . ."

Thibaut was shaking again and not from cold.

"We remain."

Chapter Two

1941

A man in a homburg hat emerged into the Place Felix Baret. He still wasn't accustomed to the quality of the noise: petrol rationing kept more and more cars from the road, and in this modern town he could hear wagon wheels and horses' hooves.

Port city, hot thug metropolis, exileville, clot of refugees, milked dry and beaten. 1941, and *France for the French*.

Varian Fry, thirty-four, thin, his mouth set, with his attention and his focus, looked like what he was: a man who knew something. He squinted at the line outside the office. He'd grown used to the terrible hope he saw in those crowds.

The alleys bustled and the bars were full enough. There were yells in many languages. The mountains still watched over everything and the late spring was warm. Streets away, the sea shifted. *I should be sitting on the quay,* Fry thought. *I should be taking off my shoes and rolling up my trousers.* Throwing stones into little waves to frustrate the fish. *I should kick my shoes into the water.*

He saw sellers of visas, information, lies. Marseille flushed.

A popular sign in a *boulangerie* said *Entreprise Fran-çaise,* by a portrait of the lugubrious marshal. Fry took off his spectacles, as if to disallow himself a clear sight at such barbarism.

"Mess your! Mess your!"

A young man in a cheap suit ran across the square. He was mustached on a baby face, and his eyebrows were so arched they might have been plucked, though his hair did not suggest much grooming. "Mess your!" he said.

"Can I help you?" Fry said in English.

The man stopped close to him and looked suddenly sly. He muttered something Fry could not make out. *Oto, adoni,* something.

"I'm no more French than you," Fry said. "*Is* that even French? Kindly cease torturing the poor language."

His interlocutor blinked. "Excuse me," he said. "I thought . . . I made a mistake. You're American?"

"You saw me in the consulate," Fry said.

"Right."

The man was almost bouncing from one foot to the other in his excitement. He glanced up at a sun like illuminated paper. He said, "That feels wrong," and Fry was startled, because he had been thinking the same thing.

"Mr. . . . ?"

"Jack Parsons."

"To give you the benefit of the doubt for a minute, Mr. Parsons, I'll assume you're merely naive." Was this man a cack-handed spy? A wheeler and dealer, what the British called a spiv? "Accosting someone in the street in Marseille right now . . ."

"Oh, gee, I'm real sorry." Parsons looked sincere. He couldn't have been older than twenty-three. "Here's the thing." He spoke quickly. "I was just in there and I saw you waltz straight past the whole damn line. I'm trying to travel, see? But they laughed in my face. Told me to get back to the U.S."

"How did you even get here?"

Parsons's eyes wandered to the *boulangerie*.

"'French Business?'" he said. "That's what it says, right? What else would it be?"

"It's informing you that it's not a *Jewish* business," Fry said. Could Parsons really be so ingenuous? In the shadows in the lee of a nearby wall was a pile of German-language newspapers. "Do you work for Bingham?"

Of all the U.S. diplomats in the city, Bingham was Fry's only ally. The others strove to keep cordial relations with Vichy. Fry, they knew, would have brought every refugee out of France, every anti-Nazi, every Jew, every trade unionist and radical and writer and thinker forced into hiding. But he had to choose. His Emergency Rescue Committee focused, not without shame, on artists and intellectuals.

As if the baker, the sewage worker, the nursery teacher didn't deserve help, too, Fry thought, many times.

"I don't know who Bingham is," said Parsons. "But listen. So. I'm wondering who's the swell sauntering right by the rest of us, and then I saw what you were carrying. Those papers . . ."

From his case Fry showed the tip of a handmade magazine he had brought to read in case of delays, a little stitched booklet. "This?" He pulled it out a little further. On its front was a hand-colored, twisted figure. Names: Ernst, Masson, Lamba, Tanning, others.

"Right! I could not believe it! I have to talk to you."

"Ah, are you an art aficionado?" Fry said. "Is that it?"

Marseille ate the guileless. The hotels Bompard, Levant, Atlantique were internment camps, extorting funds out of refugees. The Légion des Anciens Combattants terrorized Jews and Reds. The alleys belonged to gangsters. *This Jack Parsons,* Fry thought, *is trouble, whether he means to be or not.*

Fry had already had to banish Mary Jayne Gold from the ERC headquarters at Villa Air-Bel, the large dilapidated house just outside the town. He had overcome his skepticism toward a woman he first thought a wealthy tourist play-acting, but even his nurtured respect for her hadn't been enough to keep him from asking her to leave. Her boyfriend was a liability. Raymond Couraud—his nickname, "Killer," Mary Jayne insisted unconvincingly, a reference to his ongoing murder of the English language—was a young tough, a rage-filled deserter who hated almost all of Mary Jayne's friends, who associated with criminals, who had already broken in to the villa in what he later called a "prank," who had stolen from Gold herself. She was bewilderingly patient.

"Be sympathetic, Varian," Fry's friend Serge had said. "You should have known me when I was twenty."

"Mary Jayne's *nostalgie de la boue* is her business," Fry had said. "But we can't risk having him around."

Fry knew he must walk away from Parsons, but the young man muttered something and somehow Fry stayed put under that sky. Parsons looked avidly at the pamphlet Fry held. The right person might cross an ocean to buy art. Might even come to a war.

"Did Peggy tell you about us?" said Fry.

"Who's Peggy?" said Parsons. "I want to talk to you about *her*." He pointed to one name on the booklet's cover.

Fry followed his finger. "Ithell Colquhoun?"

"Now *that* is not the kind of name you forget."

"I don't know her, in fact," Fry said. "Or anything about her. And I certainly don't have any of her work to sell . . ."

"See, I *do* know about her," said Parsons. "And I was *not,* in a goddamn lifetime, expecting to see her name, any names I recognize, here. Which is why I want to talk to you."

Don't discuss anything with those you don't know. The Gestapo are watching, the Kundt Commission is in town. But there was something in Parsons's voice.

The Café Pelikan was crowded. Refugees, intellectuals, a smattering of Marseille scum.

"What do you know about Surrealism?"

Jack Parsons scratched his chin. "Art, right? Not much. Is that what she does? I know Colquhoun from kind of another context. Mr. Fry, listen." He leaned forward. "I shouldn't be here. I'm en route to Prague."

"You can't get to Prague," Fry said. "I still don't know how you even made it here."

"I just . . . made my way. And I have to keep going. I have a job to do. This goddamn war. It's like you said: in the right context you can make words do all kinds of things."

Did I say that? "I'm just a clerk . . ." Fry said.

"Come on. I know you run this committee. This Emergency Rescue Committee." Fry looked quickly around them, but Parsons was unperturbed. "Everyone in the office was talking. I know you have some place in the suburbs, and you look after people, artists, try to get them out—"

"Keep your voice down."

"I'm going to level with you." Parsons was gabbling. "I want to go to Prague because if I get there, there are some words I think I can make do things they wouldn't normally do. But now everyone's saying I *can't* get there. So there I am, wondering what to do, and I see you, and I see what you're carrying. And *that* is why I came running after you. Because I do not believe in coincidence."

Fry smiled. "I have a friend who would agree," he said. " 'Objective chance,' he'd call it."

"Uh huh? See, that person in your magazine is connected to exactly the kind of thing I'm trying to do. *Ithell Colquhoun.*" He made it sound like a bell ringing. "What's your connection?"

"One of my friends knows her," Fry said. "The one who shares your view on coincidence, in fact. She visited him last year, I believe, in Paris. It was he who made this pamphlet. I believe she's a painter and a writer. I haven't even read this yet."

"What's your friend's name?" said Parsons. "Who made that?"

With an effort, Fry did not answer. "How do you know Colquhoun's work?" he said instead.

"A kind of mentor of mine knew her. Spoke real highly of her, too. That's why you got me excited. Here's what

I'm wondering. Like I said, there's something I wanted to do in Prague. Now I'm stuck here. But what if that's okay? This guy I got a lot of respect for, well, he has a lot of respect for Colquhoun. So if she's one of these *Surrealists,* maybe they have the same kind of ideas he does. And I do. So maybe I want to talk to *them*. To your pals."

"My friend who knows her is called André," said Fry, after a long silence.

"Mine's called Aleister."

"André Breton."

"Aleister Crowley."

Chapter Three

1950

"Thibaut," the young scout had said. "They told me where you'd made your way. That you run things here." The woman was exhausted and bedraggled but uninjured, and smiling to have made it through dangerous neighborhoods to find him.

He did not see or hear her arrive at the door to the cellar where he was working, until she called him by name, gently enough not to alert his comrades above. He reached for his gun at the sight of her but she tutted and shook her head with collegial imperiousness. "I'm Main à plume," she said, and he believed her. That it was by some technique from the canon, some re-uttered poem in a novel context, that she had gained unseen entrance. He put his rifle down.

She spoke again and did not raise her voice.

"I came a long way, down rue des Martyrs, from the eighteenth, Montmartre," she said. "There's too much shit between here and the eighth. I'm glad I found you."

"I don't run things," he said.

"Well. Seems you do. It's you they wanted me to speak to, anyway."

"They?"

"They knew where you'd be," she said. "They—we—want you to join us. There's a plan."

She was vague, but almost brittle with excitement. Just beyond the edges of Paris's Nazi-controlled center, the comrades were amassing.

Thibaut had fingered the card in his pocket. "Come on," he said, "why do they want *me*?", and watched her shock when he told her at last that he was protecting the ninth.

———

Thibaut coils and uncoils the whip he took. He winds it densely around itself to make it a baton. He slaps it against his palm.

"This shouldn't work," he says. "They can't control manifs. They shouldn't have even been there. No one should go *into* a forest." He looks abruptly down, right at the pajamas he wears, about which Sam has said nothing. He has to gather himself a moment. " 'Confusedly,' " he says, " 'forests mingle with legendary creatures hidden in the thickets.' "

"Desnos," Sam says. "And that's not a warning. That's *why* I went in."

"Was it worth it? To see legendary creatures?" He intends to shame her with the question, with his bitter tone, but she smiles and raises her camera.

In the remains of the Lycée Buffon, the old classrooms are empty but for dust and the carcasses of birds. Thibaut points his rifle at Sam. She does not cower. She places her bags by her feet, like someone standing on a railway platform.

"Listen, American," he says. He tries to make his voice rough. "I'm Paris. Main à plume." *Liar,* he thinks. *I shouldn't even be here.* "I've fought devils, manifs, Nazis, collaborators, and I've killed them all." The Marseille card is in his pocket, that secret counter of rebellion. "Why were they coming after you? I told you. I've never seen wolf-tables like that, or manifs obeying Nazis."

"No? What about the *aeropittura*?" she says.

He blinks. "They hardly count," he says. Actual fascist manifs, such as those rushing futurist plane-presences, remain very few. "And they don't *obey* anyone, fascist or others, they just . . . lurch about . . ."

"Fauves?" she said. "The negligible old star?"

For a short time, art-shepherds from the Vichy curators of "Jeune France" had tried to direct the garish strutters walked out of Derain's canvases, the confusing and melancholy point of gray light self-made from lines written by a Vichy enthusiast. The presences, though, were uncontrollable and underwhelming. Thibaut has heard nothing of the crude bright fauvist figures in a long time, but the star is supposed to still haunt the streets some nights, emanating bewilderment.

"The wolf-tables are *Surrealist*!" Thibaut shouts. "You can't compare them to a poem by some stupid American, or fascist scrawls, or Derainist crap . . ."

"I've seen worse than those tables following orders," Sam says. "A huge thing ripped right out of art. Don't kid yourself the Reich can't manifest things sometimes."

Thibaut narrows his eyes. "You're wrong," he says.

She shrugs. "If all my films were developed, I could show you."

"How do you know so much about all this?"

"You're not a good interrogator. You're moving on to new questions before I've answered the first ones. Why were they after me? Remember?"

"So why *were* they?"

"No, let's skip forward, in fact. I know about all this because it's my job. I came in weeks ago. I'm from New York. I'm a photographer, and a curator."

"You came *through the barricades*?" Thibaut says. "From outside?"

"Come on. There are ways. You know that. Will you point the rifle somewhere else? I've done a decent enough job of staying out of sight, I thought. But when I was in the eighth I realized those officers were following me. With their . . . dogs. I went south through the Grand Palais. They must have followed."

Does she understand what she's saying? Boulevard Haussmann, the avenues des Champs-Élysées and de Friedland, Montaigne and George V: these and the neighboring streets of the sixteenth and seventeenth, around the Arc de Triomphe, are the Nazis' redoubt.

There are others throughout the city, of course, like the isolated forces of the tenth he'd seen scattered by the Vélo, cut off from each other, or connected by guarded lines. But the headquarters of the SS is on avenue Hoche; the Hotel Majestique is where the military high command still exercises rump power. Rue Lauriston is the headquarters of the Active Group Hesse, French Gestapo auxiliaries, the Carlingue. Those streets are patrolled by officers and the most reliable of their devil-allies.

The whole zone is on military and demonic lockdown. The few Parisian civilians within serve its microeconomy. If manifs intrude there they are pushed out or ended with relentless force.

Very rarely, one resistance group or other might infiltrate, carry out some raid—a theft, the liberation of comrades, a spectacular act of violence. The last time was years ago, and it was Paris itself the rebels had attacked.

De Gaulle had been predictably aghast by the Arc's changed configuration. When the dreams of the blast passed, the great structure was sedately on its side. The inside of its stone curve was wet, streaming with self-generated urine. A giant's pissoir.

It delighted Thibaut and all the Main à plume. To the Free French it was grotesque. They sent bombers undercover past the torture rooms, barracks, and ministries where trapped functionaries made strange fascist plans. When dawn came the Free French soldiers triggered their ordnance and with a great blurt of smoke and fire exploded the sideways Arc, showering the streets with rubble and piss.

The stones still lie where they landed, now dry. De Gaulle said he was salvaging Paris's honor.

It had been a blind, Thibaut knows, to detract attention from the failure of their earlier assault at Drancy, the camp *outside* the siege and the old city's arrondissements. The closed, mysterious horseshoe citylet repelled the Free French, to their shame.

And now this tourist claims she walked in, walked out, of that controlled zone.

"I was taking pictures," she says.

"Of what?"

"Everything. The last thing I saw was the Propagandastaffel." The censors' building, where fascist authorities oversee what remains of propaganda and art in a city where art hunts. Which is a great deal. She opens a bag and pulls out a canister of tightly coiled film. "To keep a record."

She hands him one and nods permission. Thibaut unspools it a little, lets a streetlamp outside the window shine through it. He squints at the tiny images. Occluded streets in negative. Tanks by the pyramid in Parc Monceau, firing in formation at a great sickle-headed fish, a Lam manif swimming violently in the air. A humanish pillar. Thibaut looks closer. It is a woman made up of outsized pebbles, lying down on grass, her legs languorously in the water.

Sam opens her notebook for him to see her neat English handwriting.

"A book," she says. *"The Last Days of New Paris."*

He is quite still. "What?" he manages at last.

"I'm here to put all this down." She looks at him quizzically. "You don't think this can remain, do you? It can't. It shouldn't. But it'll still be a tragedy when it ends. Don't you think this city deserves marking?"

Thibaut unrolls a few more pictures, nervous to see the images of places he has never seen, in his own city. That he is leaving behind. There is so much of it. It is a world. Can it really be finished?

He looks closely at what she is showing him—the materials of a eulogy. These are his places.

"It's hard to develop them here," Sam says. "I'm out of chemicals. The rest will wait till I'm out."

Negatives of soldiers and devils, machine-gun stations, ranks of vehicles, the Nazi zone. Embryos of a book. A first and last travelogue. "We need this," she says. "For when it's all done."

He looks at tiny offices with swastikas on their walls, their desks bursting with paper. Close-ups of those papers. How did she get in?

Here: the Palais Garnier, its stairs dinosaur bones. He squints. Le Chabanais, the walls of the great building dissolved, light glimmering through the resin that has set around suspended women and men and the opulence and billowing cloths and gilded fittings within. A vegetal puppet, stringy, composite floral thing with fleeting human face ooze-growing up boulevard Edgar Quinet. Thibaut frowns at the sight of an arm, the remains of a white statue, a broken human face six or seven feet high, lying with stern expression in a pile of foundations. Plumes of stone-dust.

Then the sweep of a gray flank. A house-sized curve. Thibaut blinks. "That's Celebes," he says.

Sam takes the film back. "Enough," she says.

"It was. You saw *Celebes*."

The most famous manif of Paris, the elephant Celebes. Like a gray-ridged stockpot the size of a warehouse, under a howdah of geometric shapes, bull-horned trunk swaying like a small train.

"I don't know," she says. "It was something. It was fast. I took a picture and ran. It was only a glimpse."

"You're here to take *pictures*?" he says eventually, as if he's sneering. As if he hadn't gazed at them. He looks longingly at the film she holds. "To take pictures for a book?"

The sun over Paris isn't an empty-hearted ring, nor black and glowing darkly. It is not the shining rubbing of a great coin, smudged as if the sky was buckled paper. It looks everyday today.

Thibaut and Sam trek through the fifteenth. Sam says she's never seen these streets, but she moves confidently, checking her books. They duck undercover at the sound of firing or demonic burning, the wrong rhythms of a manif's hooves. They pass over a coming-together of railway lines. Not knowing why, Thibaut lets her lead.

There are sounds below them. In the shadows under the bridge, black smoke hangs and discolors the ground. Sam stares. Thibaut watches its drifts. He sees that it shifts against the wind. That it takes shapes.

Fumages, smoke figures wafting in and out of presence. They bicker soundlessly over the body of a man: they rip his clothes and stain him with soot and lift him in snagging gusts.

The presences stop. They drop their corpse. They look slowly up at Thibaut and Sam, smoke heads rising. He sees hesitation in the manifs, as they watch him without eyes. He can see them overcome it, that something has changed and it will not hold them.

He says, "Move."

Sam fumbles with her camera as she starts to run. He tries to remonstrate, to speed her up, he reaches for it but she slaps him away with startling strength. Air shifts as they stumble into the fourteenth. Sam is behind him now and Thibaut turns and sees that she is kneeling in a sudden wind. She holds her camera up with one hand, the other on the ground.

The fumages have risen. They are on the bridge. His heart accelerates at the sight. They move, half in half out of coagulation, a roiling mass of smuts. They reach, and come for her.

Before he can step toward them, try to make them flinch again, the wind kicks up. It squalls right through them and the fumages struggle and start to wisp apart. They cannot coalesce. They strain to stay, but it blows hard and they dissipate in shreds and their smoke faces silently scream as they are snatched away.

Thibaut puts his hand over his eyes while the buffeting air subsides. He turns to her at last and Sam's face is blank.

"Did you get them?" Thibaut says. She looks uncomprehending and he points at her camera. She still holds it up.

"Oh. I think so."

It smells like tar on the rue Vercingétorix. Sam leads them to a black door.

Thibaut uses the strength his nightclothes give him to pull the remains of a car apart. It is so rusted its metal barely screams. He piles the pieces up into a hind. Sam unfolds a tripod and camera, points it at the door of 54 rue du Château. Mucky gray curtains cover the windows.

"So," Thibaut says. "What's here?"

"I've got a good number of manifs already," Sam says. "The horse head. The stone woman you saw. I've been to the Trocadero." The demolished music hall came back the day after the S-Blast. It contains lions. Sam grows excited as she continues her description. "But I need as many as I can get. All of them. If I'm right," she says, "something very particular gets born here tonight."

"How do you know?"

She points at her books. "I read between the lines."

When she was very young, she tells him, she wanted to be a witch. Everything she says makes Thibaut feel callow. He is sure she is wondering why he keeps her company.

She wants to tell him how she came to be caught up by the art that now makes Paris what it is.

"First it was monster pictures," she says. "Devils and bogeymen. Witches, alchemy, magic. Then from there to here. I'm hardly the first to come that way. Think of Selig-mann. Colquhoun. Ernst and de Givry? Flamel and Breton? You've read the 'Second Manifesto.' 'I ask for the profound, the veritable occultation of Surrealism.'"

"That's not what he meant by that," Thibaut says.

"He said he wanted to find the Philosopher's Stone!"

"And he said he wanted to lose it again."

They look at each other. Sam even smiles.

"From devils to Bosch to Dalí," she says. "From him to all this. To the manifestos. That's why I'm here."

She hesitates, then continues quickly. "When informa-tion started to come out after the blast, information *about* the blast, I *had* to come. You just don't know what it was like, to see that footage."

"No. I was too busy being the footage."

"I'm not suggesting it was easier for you." She looks away, at the corpse of a crow. "I was in the gallery." She sounds as if she is trying to recall a dream. "Everyone was screaming at all these crazy, jerky pictures coming out of Paris, all the manifs. '*What's that? What's that?*' And I knew *exactly* what they all were. I knew the poems and the pictures and I knew what I was looking at."

Since the blast, curators have been Virgils. Their mono-graphs and catalogues now almanacs.

"The S-Blast," Sam says slowly, "took instructions."

She finds something in a copy of *Le Surréalisme au ser-vice de la révolution* and holds it open for him. Thibaut reads, " 'On Certain Possibilities of the Irrational Embellishment of a City.' "

"They made suggestions," she says.

He's read this before, a long time ago. He reads it again: provocations, once fanciful, now true, descriptions of Paris, from years before the explosion.

"I'm lucky you heard my shots," Sam says when he sits back. "Thank you again."

"Did you find phantoms in the forest?" Thibaut says. Her calm energy is beyond him. " 'Chemical-blue, twisted machines of jujube-trees of rotten flesh'?"

"Yes," she says. "And I took their picture. They'll be in the book. I want the ruins. Soldiers. The Resistance." She takes a picture of him in his nightclothes.

"Is it not too dark?" he says.

"Not for this camera."

Thibaut breathes deep and considers. A heavy hardback. Photographs, eulogy, the nights and days of Paris after the blast. Who will write the text?

"So the Nazis saw you taking pictures and came after you," he says. "With those wolf-tables. They think you're a spy. What was it you photographed?"

Sam examines her camera. "Mostly what I want is the manifs," she says. He thinks he sees distaste when she says that, alongside her eagerness. "I'm not leaving until I catch them all."

They listen to the hooting of predators and the calls of

prey astounded to exist. From behind the ripped-up car a feathered sphere the size of a fist rolls into view, sending up dust. It opens. In its center is a single, staring blue eye.

Sam stares back at it.

"It's eating," Thibaut says. "They live on looking." It feels good to tell her things she does not know. "You can catch them and make them fat if you show them bright colors. Then we roast them." The meat was greasy with everything they'd seen. A horde of the things rolls into view behind the first. Sam takes pictures as they regard her.

Thibaut decides he will stay with her a while.

Mosquitoes come. "I heard about a cell of your people," Sam says. "A big one, maybe the main one. That there was a plan. I heard they were ambushed."

Thibaut says nothing and he doesn't look up. He continues to divide his food. He has bread and smoked meat. Sam has chocolate she says she bartered from an American secret agent on some mission of murder.

"They're all in here," she says when she sees him looking at it. "This place is crawling with that kind. They're on their own in here."

"This secret agent can't have been very secret," Thibaut says.

She laughs. "He was at first. They always tell you in the end."

When the Germans sealed the city, the U.S. government, like every, expressed its outrage. And, also like the others, was relieved. That the manifs and their energies—and, or, the devils—would be contained.

"But you can't keep this in," Sam says. "Best you can do is slow it. Things have started happening."

She tells him of the North Africa campaigns, the dragged-out misery of the Pacific, Europe after the rain. But what Thibaut wants to know most is what she can tell him about Paris. Because perhaps he has been too close to see. *The mission is vacant.*

The glow of the nearest streetlight comes up, then wanes. An animal lands on a windowsill, a winged monkey with owl's eyes. It watches them.

From somewhere there is a loud crack and it flies instantly away. The building groans like a ship.

Something is creaking within, something knocks and approaches. Something descends behind the door.

"Fold over paper," Sam whispers. "Fold it over and what might come out?"

Step step step. Sounds approach them, beyond the wood. A scratching and the slow slow click of a lock. The door swings open. Inside it is darker than the street.

Thibaut does not breathe. With a careful jerking step, something comes out of the shadow.

—

A towering, swaying thing. Three meters tall. More. It blinks with alien gravity.

It stands like a person under a great weight, swaying on two trim legs. At its waist it is made of lines, offcuts of industry. A tilted anvil-like workbench, bits and machine pieces higher than Thibaut's head. He stares up at a pole of fetish objects. A clamping bench on engine parts on patient human feet. At the top of it all, an old man's too-big bearded face looks down at him with obscure curiosity. In his beard, a steam train the size of a cudgel, its chimney venting smoke into the bristles. The old man wears a larva on his head. Some limb-long bright caterpillar, gripping an outsized leaf. It wriggles and the leaf-hat flutters, hedgerow chic.

A random totality, components sutured by chance. It stands. Thibaut stares at this thing. It looks back at him, as the first manif he ever met, its cousin, did through its helmet grill, years before.

Sam's camera clicks. "Exquisite," she whispers. For the first time, Thibaut hears fear in her voice. "Exquisite corpse."

An ugly percussion shocks them out of awe. There are shouts and shots. Out of the dark, German soldiers come running.

Thibaut ducks behind the remains of the car and fires.

Behind the attacking Nazis a jeep is rocking over the

rubble toward them. How long have these soldiers been waiting?

Thibaut fires as they come and tries to focus and counts and calculates what he can see. There are too many. His heart slams. Too many. He holds his breath and reaches into his pocket, for the card, *this time,* he thinks, *in time.*

But the exquisite corpse is striding into the road. The soldiers gape and fire. It raises its limbs and all the German bullets, even those misaimed, curve in the air, fly right into it, stud its body with resonant sounds.

Some of those shots were at Thibaut.

The soldiers have nets and strange engines. He can feel them. A lasso whips and snares the manif. In the jeep Thibaut sees two men, a thickset uniformed driver, a black-coated priest. He glances at Sam and she looks as if she is saying a prayer. Thibaut slams his rope cosh, the twisted wolf-table lash, against the ground.

The exquisite corpse leaps. For the moment of its jump everyone in the Paris street feels as if they are on the mezzanine of a snake-flecked staircase.

The world torques—

—and Thibaut and Sam and the exquisite corpse are standing a long way from where they were, meters from the Nazis. There is the silence of confusion.

The rope still snags the manif, stretching back into a now-distant engine on the jeep's flatbed. A pulley starts to grind, and the cord tightens, strains to reel the exquisite corpse in.

It tugs back like a playful horse. It turns in ancient-eyed attention to the officers of the Reich. It puffs out its cheeks and semaphores its limbs, wheezes into its beard, rips into the street with the edges of its machinery body.

A tear full of white. The edges of reality break. The Nazis stagger on the wrong side and broken bits of car crumble into that papery void.

The exquisite corpse nods, and the Nazis all lurch and fall and slide away as if it shoved them.

Sam is running away from the rip and the soldiers. Thibaut hesitates, grips with his innard sinews, and goes to the exquisite corpse. He pats it gently with the tip of the rope-cudgel.

Its body resonates under his tap like a hollow oven. It turns slowly and looks down at him with its man's head and eyes. He moves back. With skittish steps, the manif follows him.

"Come on!" Sam shouts. The Nazis fire from beyond the reknitting hole, and Thibaut spreads his pajamas into a shield, like a weaponized sail, and, the exquisite corpse behind him, he runs.

"Did you smell the exhaust from that jeep?" Thibaut says.

"Blood smoke," Sam says. "That doesn't run on petrol any more. They must've refit it with the help of demons."

"They were trying to snag this thing," Thibaut says. "Like with the wolf-tables. They're trying to *control manifs*. And they almost did."

"Not this one they didn't," Sam says. She looks back uneasily and away again. "They didn't have a hope."

It treads behind them.

Thibaut has unwound his cosh and dangled the table-wrangler's cord around one of the manif's metal extrusions, what are not quite limbs. It is not a leash—it is not taut and Thibaut would never consider pulling—but he has one end of it and the manif does not object to wearing it, and joined by the bond the living art comes with Thibaut as though he holds its hand.

It is morning, a part of the city all razed into a flat ashy vista. They are in rubble full of birdcages. Some are empty, some contain silent watchful birds. A broken screen; a litter of toys' heads cracked like shells; a motionless little girl-thing standing in her white dress and watching with a featureless hole where a child would have features. From her they keep their distance and their gazes. Far ahead of them a baby's face the size of a room protrudes from the ground like some whaleback, staring skyward. It squawls quietly. Sam takes a picture.

Beyond boxes of preserved butterflies, they see drapery hanging from trees. They hear spectral guns. This place is a shooting range haunted by ghost bullets.

"This is Toyen's landscape," says Sam.

"I know what it is," Thibaut says. "I'm Main à plume."

The exquisite corpse picks through the dust. Sam looks at it with the same expression that she wore the previous night, when she at last slowed under a balcony poised during its deliquescence, and turned and stared at the manif.

She could not stop herself rearing back at the sight, and the exquisite corpse reared, too, and stamped. In alarm, Thibaut tried to hush it, had concentrated his attention to that end. To his amazement the thing calmed.

"They don't like me," Sam said.

"Manifs?" he said. "They don't have any opinion about you."

But when he at last persuaded her to take the rope, the exquisite corpse bared its teeth, and Sam let it go.

"It seems to know *you're* an ally," she said.

Now Thibaut flexes his intuition again. The manif exhales exhaust from its beard-train. It follows him like something that knows something.

In the sky a storm of birds takes the shape of one great bird, then of a dancing figure, before they scatter. Sam takes a picture of that, too.

"I was on my way out," Thibaut says to her abruptly. "When I found you."

Sam waits.

"A while back, I met a woman *riding* a manif," Thibaut starts again.

"The Vélo," says Sam. "I heard something about that . . ."

"You heard?" Thibaut can feel the card in his pocket. "Well, I was there when her passenger died. And when I went through what she was carrying . . . I think she was a spy. Like your chocolate man."

"Naturally."

"British. SOE." Thibaut holds up the cord he carries. "She was controlling her manif with leather, too. Or trying to. We didn't keep the thong: we should've done. She had a map. With stars drawn on it, and notes."

"What did the notes say?"

A constellated Paris. They had pulled the dirty thing from her inside pocket. "Most of them were crossed out," Thibaut says. "They were the names of lost objects. They were famous manif things." Thibaut looks at her and can see she understands. "I thought maybe she was a magpie. She was artifact hunting, for sure. But perhaps it wasn't for her."

"Had she found any?"

He feels as if the playing card is moving in his pocket. "Well," he says. "She had none on her. Maybe she crossed them off when she found out they were gone."

"Or took them and passed them on."

He licks his lips. "So anyway," he says. "Eventually, we used it. The map. Of course. My comrades and I. Went looking. Went to the Bois de Boulogne."

"Why?"

"Because that was where there was a star that wasn't crossed out."

"I mean why eventually? Why didn't you go hunting straightaway?"

"Oh." He keeps his eyes on the horizon. "I persuaded them to wait." His comrades had not known what for, but they had agreed. "I'd heard something about that other plan you mentioned. Never knew the details. Just that it was some assault. I thought we should wait, see if we heard anything. In case it succeeded." She says nothing so he must continue.

"It didn't," he whispers. "It went wrong. Chabrun, Léo Malet and Tita, a lot of others. They died."

"I heard," Sam says. "Do you know what happened?"

"I think the enemy got wind of it. They hit first. And they must've had some . . . *weapon*." He bares his teeth. "I don't know exactly what but our people—it was the best of us who died. The best. The Nazis must've had something ready to go into those streets." He could, might have been there, with the now-dead. Then he would be dead, too.

Except if his presence would have changed things.

Thibaut had fought the Carlingue once, alongside Laurence Iché. A day full of flat light, the two of them patrolling, she showing the rookie the area. A routine sweep of a quiet zone. Expecting nothing, they walked into the remains of a battered lot, and an ambush.

He had hurled himself screaming for cover, trying to shoot as he went, trying to bring training to mind as he cowered under fire. When he turned and hauled himself half upright, Iché was stood there in her grubby floral dress, still smoking hard, ignoring all the bullets that crashed around her, raising her right arm.

She roared and a too-big eagle appeared and plunged straight for the men gathered at the cul-de-sac's entrance. As Thibaut cowered and watched the wings beat down on them and they gasped and tried to run she had said something else and made a caterpillar longer and fatter than a horse with the head of a wicked bird, and it rippled after the eagle over the shattered brick. Thibaut heard cries and wet noises. Iché brought a bathtub full of glimmering, shredded mirror into presence and sent it skittering on its claw feet into the slack-faced Gestapo commander. It bumped him and caught him with all its grinding scintillas. He screamed and sent up a spray of blood and reflections.

"I saw Iché manifest her own poems once," he says. "Not many could do that."

"Maybe your comrades had some secret weapon, too," Sam says. "I heard things."

"So you keep saying. I don't know. I don't know if they had what they wanted. If there was anything."

"Well, there *were* stories. About a fight. Between something manif of theirs—yours—*and* something Nazi—"

"I heard rumors, too," Thibaut interrupts, making her

blink. "If they had a secret weapon it didn't fucking work, did it?"

"Is that why you're leaving?" Sam says after a moment. He does not reply. "What was it happened in the forest?" she says. "Did you find what you were looking for?"

"I should've fucking left then," he says. "As soon as I heard about that fiasco. That they were gone. But I stayed. We all stayed. Decided to follow the map."

His cell. Around a fire. Drinking to the memory of the dead. The identities of whom they were not even quite sure. They knew, though, from the tenor of the rumors they had already heard, the transmissions in garbled code passed on by runners at arrondissement edges, reaching them at last, from the shift in the atmosphere, for those like Thibaut who could feel it, that this failed assault changed things. That a chance had been lost, for their side.

None of them slept that night, after the word reached them, word they could not be sure was true but were quite sure was true. They gathered together and talked quietly, tried to reconstruct which of the great booms across the city that they'd heard over the last week had been the noise of their comrades falling, according to what bad powers.

Those who'd known them spoke about their times with those they thought gone. He had troubled his comrades, though, because Thibaut would tell no such stories of those who'd inducted him. He would say nothing. He fingered the Marseille card and thought of the scout who had come for him, whom he had turned away.

After his refusal, that woman who had crossed such dangerous ground to find him had not spoken again. Someone else might have begged, or insisted. There was a long silence, and he made himself meet her eyes, and when at last she was certain he meant it she turned without a word and ascended the stairs.

After a second's hesitation he went after her. On the ground floor he had found Élise standing in confusion by a door that was ajar onto a backyard with a broken wall, the night and the streets, and the woman who had come unseen by any of his comrades now gone again the same way, back to whatever was being planned, without him.

Later the names. Hérold. Raufast. Rius. Iché. That sickening roll-call.

"But no," he says to Sam. "I had to leave later. After the forest." He looks down at the filthy nightdress he wears. "Yes, we found what we were looking for there. I mean, when we suspected the Brits wanted it, were after it, we wanted it more, didn't we?"

A last chance. They woke one morning and found that Cédric had left. "Screw him," Pierre had said, but they all knew they were weaker without the priest, if demons attacked. Thibaut unfolded the spy's map and proposed a plan.

———

In New Paris, Sacré-Cœur wears a clotty skin of black paint, and thrusting meters out from all its splendid vaulted windows where glass once was and its doorless doorways are shifting tram-lines. Thibaut and his crew trekked to the shadows of the ex-church, to where tracks shook like lizard tails, lashing the pavement and the roofs with a grind and whiplash of metal, moving, appearing in the fabric of the area, grinding into the ground as if they were old infrastructure, stretching abruptly out of sight, twitching to change positions, disappearing again.

Every few minutes or hours, a tram would emerge from within and howl driverless out of the cavernous interior of the church and hurtle along one or other of these evanescent tracks into the city.

The Main à plume found a place to wait, climbed a ladder of sinewy muscled arms that wriggled under their weight, to huddle in a street-corner bivouac, watching manifs that watched them back, looking out for Nazis and devils. Things were bleaker now they suspected a little of what had failed. The cobbles shifted before them to become rails. They waited and spoke little and mostly just watched the ground change, watched the wrong trams.

Until after a day and a night, Thibaut, bleary-eyed, saw one streetcar come wormlike out and roll toward them, marked on its glass front, *Bois de Boulogne*.

"Now!" he said. "Now!"

The Main à plume came out of hiding running, swinging their grappling hooks, snagging the tram like a steer as it passed.

"Jean fell." Thibaut recalls the wail and slide. "He was too slow. But the rest of us got aboard."

They leaned exultant from rattling windows as the tram hurtled over graves and sent earth and headstones flying in Cimetière du Nord. Rails appeared before it and sank behind it into the earth. It explored and they hung on within.

Into the seventeenth, rue Ganneron, savaging a way through the remains of close edifices of rues Dautancourt, Legendre, Lacroix. The vehicle's lights shone onto broken inside walls. Out again, over railways where rolling stock moldered.

"We went too fast to be caught," Thibaut says. "Even when we went past Nazis."

To their terror, the tram coiled abruptly down the stairs into the vaults of Villiers Métro station, leapt onto the older waiting track and into the tunnels. Through glints of phosphorescence and ghosts. Howling in the dark. The partisans were too fearful to be raucous until it rose and was out again.

At Porte Maillot the tracks the tram put down before it entered trees. Branches and leaves slapped the windows. They slowed. They were surrounded by the green. The engine stopped at last in a clearing, gently touching the buffers that grew to meet them out of the ground.

For two days the city fighters scouted by foot in that

dream-wood, leaving the tram for the thickets. They wandered in rough extending circles, cutting routes, checking the dead woman's map.

They caught two wolf-tables—the wild, skittish ones with foxlike parts—and used their wooden bodies to roast their flesh necks. Eating the meat of a manif was supposed to change you.

"What was it that took your comrades?" Sam says.

What monster does she think? A huge featureless manif woman holed by drawers that open to emit things? A clattering of Bellmer dolls crawling crablike on mannequin legs with ball-and-socket joints? Perhaps she imagines a squadron of devils and their Nazi invokers, SS torturers working with meters-high beasts bearded with stalactites of sulfur.

No.

They found the treasure at last, the pajamas marked by the star.

They were flapping on a hanger in a tree, dancing in the wind, watched by owls. Thibaut and his comrades paused at the sight of them in the shadowed moonlight, at the feel of them. They crept toward the gilt thread.

"I thought if they were anywhere they should have been in the Hauts-de-Seine," Thibaut murmurs. " 'My pajamas balsam hammer gilt with azure.' " He quotes Simone Yoyotte's poem, "Pajama-Speed," from the pages of *Légitime Défense*. The cloth was woven with legitimate defense. "It wasn't me getting them."

Pierre was in front, reaching for the cloth, when a shot from the trees felled him.

"We all went for cover," Thibaut says. "We'd been found. Followed. I don't know since when. We left tracks, for sure. I was right behind Pierre. I grabbed the night-clothes." He fingered their hem. "I pulled them on. So they couldn't hurt me."

What came for them out of the woods? What had tracked their incompetent scoutwork, using them to find this prize?

Not even Nazis in uniform. Not animals from art, nor howling transplants from Hell. Murderous banalities. French men and women, living by theft, killing by surprise. They jumped into sight, making what they must have thought were savage sounds.

Thibaut's first poem-enhanced punch crushed a bandit's face. Bullets pattered against him. For all his new strength, though, he saw in anguish that his comrades were dying, because he was still clumsy in these clothes.

He leapt an enhanced leap and overshot by many meters and fell down with the fight behind him. A ghastly comedy. A man knifed Bernard and another shot Brigitte in the back while Thibaut staggered and tried to come for them.

Two ambushers fell to Main à plume shots but the assassins had managed to filch a couple of Surrealist techniques, too, and as Thibaut watched, Élise cried out and was turned to cloud. He ran to gather her but she was vapor, and gone. Patrice was eaten by a flock of wooden birds at which he batted, and which he could not destroy. Thibaut struggled with his jerky strength as his comrades fell.

At last the surviving bandits ran. Thibaut sank to his knees in his armor, wearing the treasure they'd come for. He knelt among his dead.

"It wasn't demons," he says to Sam. "Nor manifs or Nazis. Just Parisians."

I am going, he told himself at last when he stood up from his grieving, his slaughtered friends around him. This was what did it, not the unseen catastrophe of his leaders. This little local murder. *I'm done. The mission is vacant.*

He set out.

I'm done with this dream.

Sam says, "I can help you get out."

Thibaut asks himself why he isn't just expending the last charge of these insurrectionary nightclothes to smash through the siege and run, to leave the ruins of Paris for the ruins of France beyond. Are these really the city's last days?

"It'll be a beautiful book," he says at last.

"You can help," she says. "I can show you how to get out. But first, I need more pictures."

He wants the book. He realizes it with slow wonder.

He wants to help with it. Thibaut has learned to obey such intuitions.

Too, he wants to know what Sam's real mission is.

He grips the exquisite corpse's cord. He does not know what it is he does, nor how, to have it follow him, but his heart accelerates. *If you'd been with us,* he thinks at it. *In that forest.*

"That SOE woman," Sam says. "You said she could make the Vélo do things."

"Well, she was trying."

"The rumors outside are there's all kinds of experiments. Not just art stuff: occult, too." She looks into the sky. "Allies working on manifs. Nazis on manifs. Allies trying to crack demons. I heard that some manif version of Baudelaire was *sacrificed* by Nazis."

Thibaut says nothing. He suspects that she's speaking of the Baudelaire of the Marseille deck, Genius of Desire. The sibling of which he carries.

"When I was coming in," Sam says, "I kept hearing that more Teufel Unterhandleren are on their way in."

These are the military specialists that cajole the pained demon refugees, with knick-knacks and incantations, according to the terms of contested treaties. They work in close conjunction with Paris's fascist church, poring over relics and books of banishment, under plaster crucified Christs wearing swastikas, with devils painted at their feet staring up in resentful thrall. "For the glory of God," Alesch has declared, "we crook his cross, and in his name we command not only his still-risen angels but those angels fallen."

His order barters with devils. Alesch's priests are not exorcists: they are anti-exorcists.

"I kept hearing all these stories," Sam says. "About new factors. About something called Fall Rot."

Chapter Four

1941

"I can't believe it." Mary Jayne Gold's voice shook. "After the trouble he gave *me*? He brings someone here we've never even met? Has he lost his mind?"

"I don't know," said Miriam Davenport. "You saw him—he's in a queer way."

Mary Jayne put her finger to her lips as Fry stomped back. He glowered at the two women. Davenport was dark and short, Gold tall and fair. An absurdly perfect juxtaposition, standing to either side of the dark wood table by bundled herbs and half-drunk bottles of wine.

"I'm sorry but it is *not* the same," he said at last. "I heard you. Mary Jayne, I'm sorry but Raymond is a *criminal*. He broke in here." Mary Jayne stood with her hands on her hips. "Whereas this Jack, this Jack Parsons . . . he's just a lost young man—"

"You have no idea who he is," said Miriam.

"He was so excited about that Colquhoun woman," Fry said.

"Whom you also don't know," said Miriam.

"No. But André told me about her. And Parsons is interested in the movement . . . I've only asked him to join us for supper." Now he beseeched. "I think he'll amuse André and Jacqueline."

"Wasn't it you who told me we can't be inviting every lost soul?" Davenport said.

"Something's coming to an end," Fry said. "Don't you feel like that?" He was startled by his own words.

He was the man who had chosen to vacate the villa himself rather than compromise it, being as he was an object of attention. The man who, in agonies, forbade his good friend Victor Serge from lodging there, deeming the communist dissenter too great a danger. Now it was Fry bringing home foundlings.

"Parsons said he was a *rocket scientist*," Miriam said.

"So he's a fantasist," said Fry helplessly. "He's harmless." He barely knew what he was saying. "I think it'll be all right. It's only supper."

———

The room in the old house was beautiful and fading. Jack Parsons looked out to the sprawling grounds, where a woman and a man chatted by the pond. Another man had climbed into a tree, was removing pictures from its branches, where they had been hung in strange exhibition.

Parsons had come to France by trains and planes, planes and boats, the pulling in of favors, the paying of bribes. And at moments, when everything had militated against him, when the timing was quite wrong, the official obstruction too implacable, when his urgent, incompetent wanderings had seemed doomed, he had asserted his will.

As many times before, in the U.S., he had flexed the muscles of the mind. As Aleister Crowley had taught him. As he whispered spells when the rockets he made went up. He was used to carefully, intensely interpreting after all such actions, to see if or how the world had responded, in if any subtle ways.

Now in Europe, no such assiduous parsing of aftermaths was necessary. Here the effects were astonishing.

He would speak commands to the universe. He would say to the train guard, "You've already seen my ticket," would strain to make himself slightly invisible to police, to make time drag enough for him to make his connections. He would have been delighted with an instant's uncertainty, a stuttering of wheels on the track. Instead the officials would usher him to a fine seat. The police would release their grip, and stand back to let him run. The train might lurch right back to where it had been three or four seconds before.

Do what thou wilt. Magic was welling up here from below. It made him feel exhilarated but sick. Its deployment made him queasy. *Maybe I can even read minds here,* he thought.

When he crossed the border, a few miles out to sea, when he came into French waters lugging his cobbled and home-tooled equipment, Jack had felt the presence intensify. Something in France was quite wrong or quite right.

He had, of course, nudged Varian Fry's mind, tweaked him to let Parsons visit.

"Let's give this one more try." Jack spoke, in his absence, to Von Karman, his boss and friend.

Theodore Von Karman took Jack to work in the Aeronautical Laboratory. Von Karman indulged and liked him, forgave him what he thought eccentricities with respectful good humor. Mostly they talked rockets and math, at first. Politics was to come. A disciple in the Ordo Templi Orientis, Jack was not accustomed to admiring the mass of humanity: Von Karman he could not fail to.

Von Karman had looked sick as news had started to emerge from Europe. "It is trouble," he said.

It was Von Karman who told Jack, without knowing that he was doing so, that there were words in Prague that might alter the storm of Europe. A presence he might invoke. Von Karman thought it only folklore. Jack, though, knew the truth, because of his other teacher. Von Karman nurtured his mathematics, the rigor of his rockets; Crowley nurtured his spirit, taught him of the other laws. One told Jack of the power in Prague; the other gave him the insight to know that it was, indeed, power.

Now Jack could not get to Prague. But now, too, there was this not-coincidence, this house of Surrealists. They, too, were faithful to revolt and objective chance. Perhaps in their presence he might find, speak words close in transmogrifying power to those he had originally sought and planned to articulate.

"They want to set free the unconscious," Fry had told him. "Desire." He shrugged. "You'd have to ask them," he added, but Parsons did not think he would. With that gloss he understood why Colquhoun would be in both this group and in Crowley's order. *Their aims were the same.*

I'm leader of the Agape Lodge. Anointed by the great wizard himself, the young scientist was Crowley's chosen. *I'm an apostle of freedom. Like these guys. Here to help my friend.*

Jack Parsons was attuned to the unholy. He could tell there was magic from Hell in the ground of France, that someone was raising. He was certain that it could help him.

So he checked his tools and dressed for dinner. When he entered the dining room, everyone turned to look, and he hesitated.

Come on, he told himself. *You're here for a reason.*

—

Painters, poets, anarchists, Reds. A poised blond woman gave Parsons her hand and introduced herself as Jacqueline Lamba. Jack nodded as politely as he could and followed her to meet her husband.

André Breton. A fleshy-faced man with sweeping hair. He looked at the young American with half-closed eyes of almost languid intensity. Parsons met the stare with his own. "I wanted to ask you something," Parsons began. "About Ithell Colquhoun."

"*Je ne parle pas anglais.*" Breton shrugged, and walked away.

Jack frowned and took a glass of wine. A slight dark-skinned man introduced himself. "Wilfredo, Wilfredo Lam." Remedios Varo, a painter, black-haired, with an intense gaze, nodded at Jack without much interest. A cool, tall woman, Kay Sage, inclined her head. Jack said hello to them all and kept watching Breton, who would not talk to him. A vivid-eyed man called Tanguy laughed too loud. These Surrealists wore battered evening clothes.

"Jack Parsons," Fry said to a small smiling gentleman, Benjamin Péret, who greeted Jack with a lopsided mouth, while Mary Jayne and Miriam watched. "He's stranded among the Nazis."

"The Nazis? You know of Trotsky?" said Péret.

"I guess."

"He says these fascists are dust that is human." Péret nodded vigorously. "He is right."

"What would they think of you, Parsons?" someone said.

They sat to heavy vegetable stew seasoned only with salt. Parsons breathed deep and drew strength from the hex-fouled land outside. *Do they even know?* he thought. *That something's happened?*

He sat in the Villa Air-Bel with the artists and radicals, writers, the *philosophers* that bleeding-heart Americans wanted to smuggle out of France. *What am I doing here?* He looked at his food in despair.

"Foreigners need to carry seven pieces of paper all the time," Mary Jayne Gold was saying. Why was she looking at him like that? Had he invited this information? Jack had lost track.

"You don't say," said Jack. "That's crazy."

"Varian says you're a scientist."

"Yeah. I work with . . ." He made his hand zoom through the air. "Rockets." *I make bombs fly with fucking Greek fire. And you will thank me.*

"Do you know our guests made a pack of cards?" Miriam said.

"I did not know that."

"Yes," said Lamba. She laughed. "We will play with you."

———

Trapped in their Marseille hinterland, this pre-exile, the Surrealists had drawn new suits, a cartographic rebellion. Black Stars for dreams; black Locks, Keyholes, for knowledge; red Flames for desire; and Wheels for revolution. They had enshrined beloveds as face-cards: de Sade, Alice, Baudelaire, Hegel, Lautréamont.

"There's talk of having them printed, eventually," Fry said with an effort.

"Play is resistance," said Lamba, with her heavy accent.

That's how you rebel? Parsons realized his disgust must show. In a town full of Gestapo, informers, fascists, fighters. *That's it?*

Breton was looking at him at last, in challenge.

"I saw two boys in town," Miriam was saying to someone. "They each had two fishing rods, crossed over their backs. Do you get it? *Deux Gaulles*—it's a pun, de Gaulle. They're stating their opposition."

Get me out of here, Parsons thought.

"What is it exactly brings you here, Mr. Parsons?" Mary Jayne was brittle. "This is a very odd time to travel."

Parsons could not keep track of the visitors, though their names and expertise and philosophical positions were all announced to him in what felt like mockery.

When, late, a thin, tough-faced young man came in,

Mary Jayne shouted with pleasure and went to him. Miriam glowered and made to rise, but Varian Fry, though he frowned at the newcomer, put his hand on hers to hold her back.

Raymond Couraud, his arm in Mary Jayne's, stared slowly around the room. Breton pursed his lips and looked away.

"I did tell André that you were asking about Ithell Colquhoun," Parsons heard Fry say. The name got his attention. Breton was nodding at him with a moment's interest. He spoke and Fry translated. "She did come to visit him a while ago. That's why he put her work in that little volume."

That was all. These people are nothing, Parsons thought. *Nothing.*

"It's bad for us," Von Karman had said to him, of his family, of the Jews of Europe. "My great-great-however-many-times-great grandfather," he had said, "was Rabbi Loew. You know Rabbi Loew, Jack? From Prague. He made a giant clay man and figured out how to bring him to life to keep the Jews safe. You know what that made him? The first applied mathematician."

Von Karman liked that joke. He repeated it often. It pleased Jack, too, but for different reasons. Von Karman was right: to make life was to speak aleph where there was silence, to add one to a zero. Jack read everything he could find on Loew, the efforts and triumphs of that devout man.

Between the trajectories of rocket falls, rainbow-shapes and gravity, between his imaginings of the screamings across the sky that he would send the Nazis, Parsons, with exhausting care and thoroughness, developed an arithmetic of invocation, an algebra of ritual. A witching plan.

I'll go to Prague, he decided at last. He checked his proofs. *I'm an engineer: I'll make an engine. I'll do the math in the grounds of the ghetto. I'll bring back this golem.*

He could do it. He looked forward to its swinging steps, its thick clay hands cleaving storm troopers, its purging of the city. That would shake up this war. *Screw it,* he thought. *I'll do it for Theo.*

And now here he was trapped in France by war and devil-science. In the room Fry had lent him, before descending, Jack Parsons had unwound the jury-rigged engine he had constructed to make his mathematics actual, to unfold the world. Batteries; sensors; an abacus; wires and circuits; transistors.

Colquhoun, Crowley's most desired and this guy Breton's collaborator, she had to be a gate, right?

But look. Look around this absurd room in this violent halfway town. Jack was among fops and artists. His time had been wasted.

Chapter Five

1950

Thibaut has always said "Fall Rot" in English: an injunction; two verbs, or a noun and a verb; seasonal decay.

"Case Red," Sam says. "It's German. I think it's something big." She watches him closely. "You've heard of it," she says.

In the economy of rumor, the partisans of Paris are always listening for stories of their enemies. Of any mention of Rudy de Mérode, of Brunner, of Goebbels and Himmler, of William Joyce or Rebatat or Hitler himself. Myth, spycraft, bullshit. "What do you know about someone called Gerhard?" Thibaut says. That name he has heard once, and once only, when the dying woman whispered it to him.

"Wolfgang Gerhard." She says it slowly. "Nothing. But I've heard of him. A Wehrmacht deserter sold me that name at the border. He said it's turning up in the chatter. Along with Fall Rot. Which I'd already heard of, Fall Rot, from a man in Sebastopol. That's a bad place now. Full of devils." She smiles oddly.

"He'd been *into* Paris, this guy, and got rich on what he brought out," Sam says. "He didn't care about Ernst, Matta, Tanning, Fini, he just wanted *things*. He had one of you-know-who's telephone, that was . . ." Her hands describe it. "A lobster. With wires. If you held it to your ear it would grab for you and get its legs tangled in your hair, but it could tell you secrets. It never said anything to me. It didn't like me. But this guy told me it once whispered to him, 'Fall Rot's coming.'"

"That's why you're here," says Thibaut. "To find out about this *Fall Rot*. Not to take photographs." He feels betrayed.

"I *am* here for photographs. For *The Last Days of New Paris*. Remember?" She is playful in a way he doesn't understand. "And to find a few other things out, too. A bit of information. That's true. You don't have to stay with me."

Thibaut beckons the exquisite corpse through the dust of ruins. Sam flinches at its approach. "They're chasing you," Thibaut says. "You got a picture of something that got the Nazis worked up enough to track you. What is it has them so worried?"

"I don't know," she says. "I have a lot of pictures. I'd have to get out to develop them to figure it out and there's more to photograph first. I can't leave. I don't know what's going on yet. Don't *you* want to know about Fall Rot?"

What Thibaut has wanted is out. To outrace those who follow, now maybe to find whatever image in Sam's films holds some secret Nazi weakness, to use it against them. But to his own surprise something in him, even now, stays faithful to his Paris. He's buoyed by the thought of Sam's book, that swan song, that valedictory to a city not yet dead. He *wants* the book, and there *are* pictures to take. When he tries to think of leaving, Thibaut's head gets foggy. It's madness, but *Not yet*, he thinks, *not before we've finished*.

The book is important. He knows this.

He imagines an oversized volume, bound in leather, with hand-drawn endpapers. Or another, rougher edition, rushed out by some backstreet press. Thibaut wants to hold it. To see photographs of these walls on which the crackwork whispers and scratch-figures etched with keys shift; of the impossibilities he has fought, that now walk with him.

Are they hunting images, then, as well as information about Fall Rot? Whatever else, Thibaut decides, yes, they are.

He follows Sam north over a spill of architecture. Refit

vehicles still line the streets, too-big sunflowers push their way through buildings, a quiet partisan leans cross-armed over a rifle in a top-floor window, watching them. She raises her hand to Thibaut in a wary salute that he returns.

Sam photographs. They sleep in shifts. At dawn a great shark mouth appears at the horizon smiling like a stupid angel and chewing silently on the sky.

Women and men committed to no side, to nothing except trying to live, have taken up paving stones and plowed up earth underneath. They farm amid changeable ruins, fighting Hellish things and feral dreams. They have made front-room schools for their children in townlets of a street or two, keep barricades up.

One such is close to where a house has gone. By their path, where the cellar was, the hole has filled with sodden grit. Thibaut slows here, can feel something. He stops Sam. He points. There are wet bones in the pit.

The travelers stay still and something twitches in the sludge. Snares of tubular parts tangle, untangle and rear. Water falls with a rushing sound away from a big vicious elliptical head rising, now the ambush has failed.

It is a sandbumptious, an ugly thing torn from an English painting. It eyes them with eyes on bobbing stems. Judging by the remains around it, it eats stragglers and scrawny horses, like most of its kind.

Sam takes a picture of the predator rising in the muck,

and hissing. When she's done, Thibaut braces his rifle on the remains of a wall. He focuses from his core.

His aim is not very good, but his focus can enhance his fire, his techniques are powerful, and the proximity of the exquisite corpse helps him. When he shoots his bullets slam into the hole and its inhabitant and the wallowing animal bleats and all in a rush, a single flame, at the wrong scale like the tip of a giant matchhead, takes it and goes out.

There is a burnt-out smell. The manif is dead.

As Thibaut and Sam walk on someone shouts "Hey!"

Wary faces rise into view above the nearby barrier. A tough-faced woman with her hair under a scarf throws Thibaut a bag of bread and vegetables. "We saw what you did," she says.

"Thank you," says a younger man in a flat hat, looking down his shotgun, "and no offense, but fuck off now, and stay away." He watches the exquisite corpse.

"This?" Thibaut says. "It won't cause you any trouble."

"Fuck off and keep your Nazis away."

"What? What did you call me?" Thibaut shouts. "I'm Main à plume!"

"You'll bring them here!" the man shouts back. "Everyone knows you're being hunted!" Sam and Thibaut look at each other.

"You heard of Wolfgang Gerhard?" Sam shouts. The young fighter shakes his head and gestures them away.

The wind explores the buildings. They hear firefights in distant streets. Thibaut and Sam descend a series of great declivities cracked in the pavement, that Thibaut realizes are the footprints of some giant.

Near the boulevard Montparnasse, Sam checks her charts and journals in the hard sunlight. An old woman watches Thibaut from a doorway. She beckons and when he comes to her, she hands him a glass of milk. He can hear a cow lowing in the cellar.

"Careful," she says. "Devils are around."

"For the catacombs?" he wonders. Their entrance is nearby, by the tollhouses called the Barrière d'Enfer.

She shrugs. "I don't think even the Germans know what they're doing. The observatory's close," she says, "and it's full of astronomers from Hell. Round here when they look through the telescopes we see what they remember."

The milk is cool and Thibaut drinks it slowly. "Can I do anything for you?" he says.

"Just be careful."

In Place Denfert-Rochereau, the Lion of Belfort has disappeared from its plinth. Surrounding the empty platform where the black statue used to stare stiff-legged are now a crowd of stone men and women, all with the heads of lions.

Thibaut is happy among those frozen flaneurs. The exquisite corpse murmurs beside him.

Sam is agitated. She won't or can't come close, will only just enter the square. She takes pictures of the motionless crowd from the edge and watches him with a curious expression.

Élise, Thibaut thinks. *Jean. You should be here.* For the first time since the Bois de Boulogne he feels as if he is somewhere that he has fought for.

He should have played his card. *I killed my friends,* he thinks.

What treachery against the collectivism, the war socialism of the Main à plume, keeping the card for himself. He doesn't even know what it would have done. But play is insurrection in the rubble of objective chance. That was the aspiration, the wager of the Surrealists trapped in the southern house.

"Historians of the playing card," Breton said, "all agree that throughout the ages the changes it has undergone have always been at times of great military defeats." Turn defeat into furious play. The story had reached Paris with its manifs. Breton, Char, Dominguez, Brauner, Ernst, Hérold, Lam, Masson, Lamba, Delanglade, and Péret, purveyors of the new deck. Genius, Siren, Magus usurping the pitiful aristocratic nostalgia of King, Queen, and Jack. Père Ubu the Joker, his spiraled stomach mesmeric.

The cards were made and lost, and sometimes found

again. If the war stories were true, a bird-faced Pancho Villa, Magus of Revolution, played by some Gévaudan militant, had saved his fighters from demon-baiting soldiers. In 1946, the cephalopod heads of Paracelsus, Magus of Keyholes, rose from the Seine and sank two Kriegsmarine ships. Freud, Carroll's Alice, the Ace of Flames, de Sade, Hegel, a beetle-faced Lamiel are rumored to be loose.

Thibaut carries the Siren of Keyholes. Victor Brauner's work. That double-faced woman in snarling jaguar stole. Drawn on paper but transferred by some force, scribbled lines, unfinished and all, to a card.

But Thibaut is too cautious a player. He trudges in guilt. He walks with the exquisite corpse, avatar of mad love, in a week of kindness.

"Tonight," Sam says. They bivouac in a preserved café. "There's another picture I need to take."

Thibaut looks up through the unbroken window and struggles to speak. "How about a picture of that?" he says at last.

The stars are wheeling far faster than they should. The sky is dark gray, the stars yellow, and they are not the stars of earth. They are alien clusters. Abruptly and from nowhere Thibaut knows each constellation—the Alligator, the Box without Locks, the Fox-Trap. They shift in all directions.

Sam is smiling. "The devils must be looking through the telescope," she says. "It's like that woman said." He didn't know she'd heard her. "That's the sky over Hell. They must feel nostalgic," Sam says. "There's no gate here. It's hard for anything more than scraps to get in or out. To Hell, from Hell, I mean. All the demons can do is look."

"Do you have any pictures of devils?" Thibaut says. Sam smiles again.

There are lost Nazis in the Jardin du Luxembourg. Men who sob at some depredation, mesmerized by the Statue of Liberty in the grounds. Its head is gone, just a knot of girders, its up-thrust right hand a gnarl. Protruding from the iron chest is a corpulent flesh eye. It blinks. One soldier calls out a prayer, in German, then French. He is hushed by his comrades.

Thibaut and Sam creep by them in the hedgerow. The exquisite corpse fades in and out of their company, always returning. It accelerates through the overgrowing gardens, through thickets and rosebushes, its caterpillar rearing, to where tall railings at its edge are spread like the tines of a ruined fork.

Night comes with gunfire. The beige and black shutters of rue Guynemer are bloody. Sam does not take rue Bonaparte but smaller streets, away from the lights and engine sounds of someone's excavations. The Bureau of

Surrealist Research is nearby—long-closed but haunted
with emanations from those early experiments, cabinets of
juxtaposed equipment. The exquisite corpse is energized
here.

This is a contested zone. In the rue du Four they hide at
the sounds of shouted German. "There are bases nearby,"
Sam whispers. The Hotel Lutetia where Nazi officers are
stationed, the Prison du Cherche-Midi where political
prisoners become experiments and food for terrible things.

"Where are you taking us?" Thibaut says. When he sees
the spire of a church at the end of rue de Rennes, he
abruptly knows the answer.

"You can't get in," he says. He wants to be wrong.

"Neither can you," Sam says.

Two of the five corners of the junction they reach have
slid into building-dust. Where rue de Rennes meets
Bonaparte, a great rock, like something split from a moun-
tain, hangs just above the ground. The church of Saint-
Germain-des-Prés is still a church, and it looks untouched.
And there, on the fifth corner, is Les Deux Magots.

The café's green awning flaps frantically, pushed out-
ward by a rushing wind from within. Around it are tables
and chairs, all heaving up and suspended as if about to fly
away, then spasming back to their positions on the ground.
Up again, head height, and back. As they have jumped for
years.

The windows are blown out repeatedly, surrounded by
broken glass that twitches and snaps back into the panes

then out again, repeatedly, an oscillating instant of combustion. The café rumbles.

Sam walks heavily toward it, into the empty road around it. It looks as if the air exhausts her, as if she walks against a gale. She stops, gasping, still meters from the entrance. The air rushes in Thibaut's ears.

It was from here that the S-Blast came.

And in all the years since, this famous ground has been impenetrable. No one has been able to push through the windless windlike force it extrudes, its own memory of its explosion.

"I know you want a picture," Thibaut shouts. "But how can you get *in* there . . . ?"

She points.

The exquisite corpse is walking forward. Continuing where they can't. The old-man face sniffs the air, the steam train's plume streams backward. It recognizes this place, some stink of something here.

Thibaut's insides are boiling. Sam shoves him after the manif. It strides without effort through the outer fringe of glass.

"That thing won't let me get close to it," she says. "*You,* though . . ."

"I can't take your picture for you!"

"I don't want a fucking picture, you fool," she says. "There's something *in* there. Bring it *out.*"

What? What is she asking me?

Am I doing this? Thibaut thinks. *I can't be.*

But not only is he grabbing the cord that trails the ground behind the manif, and winding it around his wrist, to link himself to the exquisite corpse, but now he is running, shoving his way toward it, putting his hands on its metal body.

Thibaut is drunk on whatever streams out of that place. He walks with this most perfect manif, this ambulatory chance, like the towering exquisite corpse on the grounds where his parents died, that first manif he ever saw, a terrified boy, that would not hurt him.

Glass shatters unendingly but Thibaut is safe and can force himself on in the corona of the manif's presence. They pick their way together between tables and chairs, pushing, Thibaut gasping in hot air, into Les Deux Magots, inside.

A room full of darkness and light, glare and black, heat and soot, and Thibaut can hear his own blood and the drumming of wood. His face streams with heat. His eyes itch. The tables are dancing on their stiff legs. They somersault endlessly at the point of an explosion.

There are bodies. Skeletons and dead flesh dancing, too, in the same blast, meat ripping from bones and returning to them. The exquisite corpse steps like a dainty child through a carnage of burning waiters, and Thibaut follows, fighting for breath, on his mission again.

The kitchen is full of a storm of burst plates. At its center is someone long-dead. He is a ruin.

A tough, wiry young man, whose glimpsed face snarls and burns up and whose bones burst from him in twitching repetition, his grimace dead pugnacity then dead pain then the rictus of just death, again and again, too fast to follow. He moves like a blown-up rag doll as fire and devilry and shrapnel flay him in a cloud of shards. His hand is on a metal box, it blossoms extruding wires, paper, light. It, too, bursts forever.

Out of it comes, had come, would come the blast.

The exquisite corpse trembles, this close to the point. A dream straining against what made it into flesh, reaching, with limbs like industry, for the bomb.

As it takes the exploded box from the hand of the dead exploder, Thibaut hears Sam scream his name.

Going out is so much faster. The manif and Thibaut half run, half fly.

Sam is waiting as close as she can come. She shouts in delight to see them reemerge. As they approach her she shouts again, eager and loud, at the sight of what the exquisite corpse carries.

But the bomb is strewing parts as it comes, and nothing is happening.

The box is collapsing and the explosion does not. Behind them the room continues to blow endlessly apart.

Thibaut and the manif run into the last of the light and

Sam stands in the road with her camera out and Thibaut realizes there is a wall of smoking thorns around her, a defense from somewhere, already withering, and at the edge of the junction, Thibaut can see Nazi soldiers gathering.

Something is coming. The street trembles. There is a booming as if things are falling out of space.

"Give it to me!" Sam bellows as they run.

But the box is still dropping components and wires and now its case is falling apart. Sam reaches toward the manif she does not like to touch, grabs it from the exquisite corpse's hand.

It scatters into nothing, and is gone. Sam screams a long scream of rage.

Mortars streak over them and take down buildings to block their way. Sam and Thibaut veer. The exquisite corpse does things to physics and they blink with the twists, and ahead of them now is the river and in it the Île de la Cité, and they keep running east along the riverbank on the Quai des Grands Augustins and across from where the Palace of Justice once was and where there is now a channel of clear water that spells something from above, and where sawdust swirls from the windows and doors of Sainte-Chapelle, a landscape of choking drifts and sastrugi at the island's edge.

The exquisite corpse is ahead of them. It lurches left

onto the Pont au Double, leads them over the bridge. It is as if Paris ushers them in. To the island, to where Notre-Dame looms.

Since the S-Blast the squat square towers to either side of its sunburst central window have been industrial silos, tall and fat, crudely hammered metal. One seeps bloody vinegar from imperfect seals: the air they enter is full of its sour stink, the ground below wet and fermented. Through the wire-strengthened windows of the other tank is a thick pale swirl. It's said that it contains sperm. Thibaut has often begged the sky to bomb it.

He barely sees it now. The manif takes them right, through the tangled wasteland of the gardens behind the church, and there at the furthest tip of the islet the Pont de l'Archevêché back over to the south side and the little bridge to neighboring Île Saint-Louis are both gone. Nothing but rubble in the river. There is nowhere to go.

They turn. The mud shudders. "They've found us," Thibaut says.

Out of the darkness by the buttresses of Notre-Dame comes a dreadful thing.

"Christ," Sam says. She lifts her camera. She looks almost exultant with fear. Thibaut shouts without words at what approaches.

A walking jag, a huge, broken white shard.

Aryan masterlegs, muscled in that Reich way, kick up

dirt. At the height of a third storey is a waist, above which is what is left where a great body broke, a crack and a massive headless ruin. The right side is a crumbling stone slope, the left the remains of the torso that ascend to an armpit where one stump of biceps still swings.

At the thing's feet scurry Wehrmacht and SS men. A familiar jeep in a gust of scab-colored smoke.

"What in hell is that?" Thibaut shouts. *Fall Rot?* he thinks. Is this staggering splinter the project?

"Nothing in Hell," Sam says. "It's a manif. A breker-man."

"Breker?" shouts Thibaut. *They got one of his to move?*

Arno Breker's looming, kitsch, retrograde marble figures stare with vacant stares of notional mastery. Uber-mensch twee, even in Paris they have all always been stubbornly lifeless, Thibaut has thought. But these legs are stamping closer.

Once it must have been a white marble man taller than a church, clapping stone hands; now it is cracked and split and half gone and still walking. Can living artwork die? Can it live, before it does?

"They got it upright again," Sam whispers.

"Again?"

The camera clicks. The ruins of the brekerman rock back as if the sound has buffeted it. It steadies itself with its half-arm, comes forward. It stamps down trees and begins to run.

The soldiers follow, rifles up. The jeep chutters. In it is

the driver they saw before and the man in full church rega-
lia, two others in plain clothes. This time Thibaut can see
the priest's heavy, lined, debauched face, and he knows it,
from news reports, from posters.

"Alesch," he shouts. Alesch himself. The traitor-priest,
head of the city's demon-tilted church.

The foot soldiers run at Thibaut and Sam and the exquisite corpse. The broken Nazi manif comes.

Thibaut fires a useless shot. The stone legs raise a stone
foot. He gazes dumbly up at it and sees that the thing is
most lifelike on its underside, all folds, verucas, gnarls. It
stamps. He leaps with pajama-aided bravery. His skirt
parachutes and the filthy fabric flaps. Bullets hit him but
the cotton hardens.

He shoots midair. Not at the broken manif but past it,
and over the infantry, at the jeep behind them all. The
driver jerks and spurts blood, and as the car veers the exquisite corpse reaches from somewhere and hauls Thibaut
back from danger, taking his breath all out of him. It
huffs, and the two closest soldiers fold away with wails
into nothing, leave pencil sketches of themselves where
they were standing. Thibaut sees the jeep spin and spray
earth and slam with an ugly burst of metal into the
church's side.

Those brekerman legs run forward and with a great
swing, kick the exquisite corpse in the center of its pile-up
self. The Surrealist manif staggers mightily and sways and
sheds bits of itself. Things wheel in the black sky.

Sam is behind an outcropping of wall, pinned by fire and blasts of Gestapo magic. She is aiming her *camera*, again, and Thibaut sees that what goes between it and the soldiers is a jet of bad energy. She takes their picture and blows them away. She takes a picture of the brekerman legs, too, but they brace against the impact and stand tall and come for her.

Coldly, suddenly, watching the broken brekerman withstand and the onslaught of the soldiers, Thibaut knows that even with whatever it is Sam deploys with her lenses, despite the wordless solidarity of the exquisite corpse, they will lose this fight.

From his pocket he pulls the Marseille card. And plays his hand.

The Siren of Keyholes becomes. Between Thibaut and the soldiers and the staggering Nazi manif is a wide-eyed woman, in smart and dated clothes. She is not like a person. The lines of her are not lines of matter.

She gabbles. Thibaut is staring at a dream of Hélène Smith, the psychic, dead twenty years and commemorated in card, glossolalic channeler of a strange imagined Mars. The inaugurated thought of her, her avatar invoking a spirit in a new suit in a new deck. Keyholes for knowledge. She writes in the air with her finger. Glowing script appears in no earth alphabet.

German bullets spray away from her like drops. Smith's

letters crackle and in the sky there is a rushing. The night clouds race. A fiery circle is coming down, coming in, a dream's dream, a manif of manif Smith's conjuration of a Martian craft, spinning.

Behind the suddenly stationary marble legs, Thibaut can make out the priest and another man stumbling from the smoking car. They retreat, supporting each other, further and further back as he aims at them, getting away from him, out of sight, and though he fires Thibaut cannot pay any more attention, because now the cartomantic Smith is pulling into presence the crafts of more Martians and troll-like Ultra-Martians. Her extra-terrestrial contacts exist, at last, in this moment, and they are descending, tearing into the air, firing. The Smith-thing exults.

Bolts burn, twist, melt metal. Fire descends and holes the earth. A fusillade out of the sky engulfs the Nazis and their smashed manif giant. There is a sound and light cataclysm.

And, at last, quiet and dark.

The sky is empty. Smith is gone. The card is gone. The wet towers of Notre-Dame quiver. Vinegar spurts where one's seams are buckled.

Where the dream Martians attacked, the ground has become a glass zone. Dying people twitch between the brekerman's feet. The legs are pulverized, the marble feet charred. They do not twitch. They sink slowly into vinegar mud.

Sam runs past the exquisite corpse. It trembles, wounded but upright. She is taking pictures, touching things, prodding smoking remnants. Her camera is a camera again. She reaches the buckled car and without seeming effort wrenches open the door by where the driver lolls. She rummages within.

"Look," she calls to Thibaut.

"Hold on, be careful," he says. She yanks a smoking briefcase from the man in the passenger seat and holds it up so Thibaut can see on it the letter K. She holds up something else, too, something twisted, three broken legs like another, wounded, Martian.

"It's a projector," she says as he approaches.

The passenger is pinioned and crushed, spasming and breathing out gore across an absurd little imitation Führermustache. He is trying to speak to the driver. "Morris," he breathes. "Morris. Violette!" The driver's uniform is a man's but she is a broad, muscular woman, now a dead ruin filling her bloodied Gestapo clothes. The passenger turns his head, shaking, watching the exquisite corpse as it approaches.

"The priest," Thibaut says to Sam. "He got away." With his other plain-clothed colleague. Moved by some uncanny means. "Sam, that was *Alesch*. The bishop. The traitor."

The jeep is pouring off bloody smoke. Sam pulls documents from the wreck, more dirty objects, the remains of machines. "Well, he went too fast," she says. "Left stuff behind." She pulls out a smoking canister full of film.

"What did you do?" says Thibaut. He kneels, speaks almost gently to the passenger, whom he can tell is dying, too, who stares with widening eyes at the case Sam took from him, at the letter K. "You can control manifs, now? Is that your plan?"

The man wheezes and bats weakly at him as Thibaut goes through his pockets and finds and reads his papers.

"Is that your plan, Ernst?" Thibaut says. "Herr Kundt?" Sam stares at the man, at that. *"What is Fall Rot?"* Thibaut says.

The passenger coughs through his blood. *"Sie kann es nicht stoppen . . ."* he says. *You can't stop it.* He even smiles. *"Sie eine Prachtexemplar gestellt."* *They made a—* something.

"A specimen," says Sam. "A good specimen."

"A specimen?" Thibaut says. "Of what?"

But the man dies.

Chapter Six

1941

Jack Parsons was drunk.

The Surrealists were playing a game. He watched them sourly. Varo drew a snake coiled on a wheeled cart. She scribbled it in seconds. From where he was sat, Jack alone could see what she was drawing.

"*Allons-y,*" she said. She held it up and turned it around, for one second, to show it to Lamba, who drew her own quick version. Which she showed to Lam, who showed his own rendition to Yves Tanguy, and so on. The glimpses were diminishing echoes, evolving from corkscrew serpent on its chariot to a spiral on a square.

The frivolity disgusted him. But though Parsons could not say why, watching excited him.

His hosts played games of whispering, hearing and mishearing each other's words. They played games of attention and chance. They played games of absurdity and misunderstanding. Fry watched with affectionate interest; Miriam with fascination. Mary Jayne smoked in the doorway, her arm around Raymond. He radiated disdain.

The games produced strange figures, and sentences that made no sense but that too made Parsons's breath come quick. *Do what thou wilt.*

The Surrealists drew and hid what they drew, folded paper to obscure it. They passed their papers around and added to each other's unseen images. Watching, Parsons breathed out in time to a gust of wind that rattled a forgotten painting in a tree's canopy outside.

Oh, he thought with a rush, as they passed their papers again. Each drew a head and hid it and passed it; each drew a body and passed it again; each drew legs or a base. *Oh, I get it. I get it.*

He rocked in his chair. He understood the link between *his* Colquhoun, the occultist, the hermeticist, tapper into the world's backways, and the Colquhoun close to this austere, courteous Breton. The connection of the golden dawn and animals and pleromic beyond to the woman committed to the liberation of dreams.

From an overlap in the middle of a Venn diagram, Colquhoun watched him.

Maybe, he thought, in the suburbs of this oppressed

town, this edge of an edge, maybe at this moment in a room full of the stateless, in a nation from which they wanted out, maybe here while they played foolish games to thumb their noses at perpetrators of mass murder, maybe an engine that he had built to do the math to make a clay man walk, to make words and numbers intervene as presences, might tap something else, too. Something that might trouble the Nazis.

"I know a game," he said. No one looked at him.

He ran upstairs, returned with all his mechanisms. The Surrealists were on another round. Parsons watched them draw while he connected cords to batteries and muttered powerful words.

"What are you making?" Fry said, looking at the mess of mechanics. "Is that art?" He looked triumphantly at Miriam. The Surrealists kept passing their papers.

"Right," said Jack. "It's an art thing." He turned switches, he checked gauges. He placed crystals, vacuum tubes, bits of paper at strategic places in the room. "Wait, just one second. Just a moment. Before you all unfold."

The Surrealists looked up in mild surprise. They did as he asked. Jack held his breath and nodded and wired up the wood and metal box at the center and turned a final switch.

Static came rushing through them all. Breton frowned, Lamba laughed, Varo showed her teeth. Everyone looked at Jack Parsons.

And he gasped as they opened their papers because he had already understood what the game was, how it worked, what it would unveil. The artists flattened out what they held, and what they had drawn, in planless collaboration, were impossible things.

Figures neither evolved nor designed. Coagula of fleeting and distinct ideas and chance. Parsons's battery clicked. The room began to fill with something unseen.

These weren't demons they'd drawn, not the goats and beasts of Hell. They were objective chance, chimeras for this era.

Jack saw a figure with the head of a singing bird, its body a clock with the pendulum swinging, its legs a mass of fish tails deftly done in pen and ink. A sketched-out bear face on a coffin, walking on clown's feet. A mustached man, rendered as if by a child, his body a buxom leopard's, rooted like a plant. Exquisite corpses, tasting new wine.

The artists laughed. The needles on the gauges swung as Parsons's battery filled. He could feel energies coiling out of these heads, these drawings, this room, into his wires.

It wasn't just drink making people giddy now. Not just the exquisite corpses they drew, nor any other game. It was the sense of something ending, a shutter closing. A noose—yes—tightening. A last song.

They played again, made beasts of collective unconscious. It grew darker with every round. Outside the trees waved their twig fingers as if clutching for art. They gave up wood memories. Parsons could feel the images that had hung from them slip into his machine.

He blinked rapidly, glimpsed things fleet past him, glimmers, presences as if from the Surrealists' papers, their games. No one else looked up.

The room was filling with history, with this ebbing movement, of Surrealism, of Marx and Freud and coincidence, the revolution of cities, liberation, and the random. Knowledge poured out of everyone and left them still knowing, and drunker, their defenses down.

And in the hills where he hid, Hans Bellmer shook. His dolls and his inkwork charged the battery. Marc Chagall dreamed and the needles spasmed. On her island, Claude Cahun looked at Suzanne Malherbe with utter urgency and they shared anger and love, a determination. A thread stretched from each of them to the Villa Air-Bel.

Around the world, the dreams and images, the work of all these women and men, the rage of Simone Yoyotte and the Martinican rebel students, the fury and delight of Suzanne and Aimé Césaire, the fascinations of Georges Henein, the red chaos of Artaud, the imaginings of Brauner, the constructs of Duchamp, of Carrington, of Renée Gauthier, of Laurence Iché, of Maar and Magritte, Étienne Léro, Miller and Oppenheim, Raoul Ubac and Alice Rahon, Richard Oelze and Léona Delacourt and

Paul Nougé, Paalen, Tzara, Rius, of hundreds of women and men never heard of and never to be heard of but who were the spirit of this spirit, the inspirations behind and unsung practitioners of this ferocious art, echoed in France. Rushed in. Through the glass. Into Jack Parsons's battery.

The older work of renegades, the poems of Aragon before his capitulation to the man of steel. The heroes of the past breathed dead breath into the machine, the singer of *Maldoror*, Rigaut, the ghosts of Rimbaud, the ruminations of Vaché, which never went away, had never gone and never would and which were always and forever part of France, all flared up like tracer bullets. And came down again, plugholing into a collection.

Into the machine.

The box hummed like a wasp; otherwise the room was quiet. People came slowly back from wherever they had been.

Everyone blinked except Raymond. He stared at the box.

Mary Jayne sighed. "Did you enjoy yourself?" she said.

Parsons laughed. "Oh yeah," he said. His voice shook. "It was terrific. Thank you for having me."

Breton closed his eyes. "This," he said in French, "was an excellent night."

"We're glad you came," said Varian Fry to Jack.

"Me, too. More than I can say."

Jack listened to French night birds. Here he was in the moonlight with a battery full of distillate, of this overlapping thing, this Surrealism. That was a freedom right there.

Parsons knew how to take a substance, render it, burn it and use it.

What can I power with this? he thought. He would build a freedom machine. *Home,* he thought. *I'll tell Von Karman. We'll build a new rocket. Armed with this. We'll blow that fucking Reich away.*

In the early morning Miriam and Mary Jayne sat in the garden drinking ersatz coffee, full of shyness they could not explain. They prodded the grass with their toes.

They heard Jack Parsons's first shout and looked up. He raised his voice and bellowed again and hammered on the window with his fist.

They ran up the stairs and entered his room to see him tousled and undressed and screaming. Aghast, throwing clothes out of his suitcase, looking for the battery.

Which was not there.

Chapter Seven

1950

At the corner of rue du Faubourg and boulevard Poisson-nière, there is raucous music. Accordian and piano and a violin play a Jewish air into the city. The Rex rises into dark clouds, its sign peppered with bullets and still glow-ing.

"Who was he?" says Thibaut.

"The man in Les Deux Magots?" Sam says. "A crook. A thief. Just a murderer. It doesn't even matter any more. I thought, we thought, if I could . . . That the box might be a way to open the city. Open gates and send messages. Out and . . ." She glances down. "But no. The S-Blast came out of that box and it's here now."

"Alesch was there," Thibaut says. Sam says nothing. "And someone else."

She says nothing.

"What's going on?" Thibaut says.

"I don't know. Truly," she says. She holds up burnt documents and the canister of film. "Fall Rot," she says. "They mention it in here, but it's oblique. It's all code words and hints, but I think they're talking about the devils. And I don't know why. That was *Kundt*. His commission used to hunt the artists, and I think after the blast, they started hunting the art. Turned into manif specialists." She looks at him. "I told you the Nazis are getting better at manifs. And now the K Commission are working with demonologists. Alesch's church."

She opens a charred file. Her lips move as she reads the half-sentences that are all that remain. "They're saying the devils should be *aspects* of something. And there's something they want to manifest but they can't, it needs more than they have . . ." She hesitates. "They're trying to do something, Thibaut. They want something."

The exquisite corpse's beard-train whistles. This cinema is a stronghold of the Free French and their allies, no friends of Main à plume, and Thibaut focuses his mind, pleading with the manif silently for silence. Every time he communicates with the exquisite corpse—because that is what this is, communication—he hears nothing back but a tone like tinnitus.

"Stay," Thibaut says. He pulls the cord. The exquisite

corpse sinks to the pavement on the corner, becomes as architecture.

The Rex's guards search them and incompetently question them and let them in to noise and warmth and the smell of drink, dirt, and sweat. Rows of seat-stubs slope down the tumbling hall. People are dancing. Women and men watch the huge screen from a raised half-floor above. What is showing is snips of images, monochrome light. Someone in the projection booth is stringing bits together, grabbing ripped-up centimeters of whatever film is by their fingers and running it for seconds, then replacing it. Melodramas, old silent movies, entertainments, news, documentary footage.

Surrealism comes for us all, Thibaut thinks.

He takes off his cap and tidies his ruined pajamas. No one looks at them: his true affiliation is dangerous here, but even the most austere Free French would not forbear deploying so powerful an artifact, Surrealist or not. Splendid figures sit in dark corners in pre-war clothes. A black woman plays chess urgently against herself. The dancers' steps raise dust.

Tattered Free French uniforms, the grimy workers' clothes of other partisans, with clues so Thibaut can judge that this person is Francs-Tireurs et Partisans or Groupe Manouchian, this one Confrérie Notre-Dame, this Armée Juive, that Ceux de la Libération. This thin intellectual from the Groupe du musée de l'Homme, perhaps; or a scout come in from the Société de Gévaudan, the legendary resistance center in a Lozère sanatorium. There might even be foolhardy rightists here, Vichy-loyal anti-Nazis. *Vichysto-resistant,* he thought them. An epithet from the future. But no Main à plume.

These streets will be bombed. Maybe trodden on by another angry sculpture, he supposes, or pulled toward Hell by fretful demons. Until then, at the end of the world, there's drinking and dancing, moonshine and crude cocktails made from remnant liquor. Behind the bar are pinned scores of IOUs: no one is sure how money works any more. On the walls are posters, memories of resistance victories. The remnants of a swastika have been allowed to stand, so that they can be repeatedly defaced.

"Watch the screen," says Sam.

"We should not be here," Thibaut says.

"So we'll be quick. We have to know. You got another projector we can use?"

She runs for the stairs. Thibaut watches the film over the heads of the dancers. After a minute it jerks and brightens. He imagines Sam shoving aside whoever is upstairs. Pistol to the head. Taking over from whoever feeds it bits and pieces of old film.

The screen goes dark then light.

Now it shows scattering airplanes, a long shot of dancing. A dim shape, in a vast chamber. Sunlight comes through a big window. There is a jump and Thibaut sees another corridor. He can barely make out the images through the distortion of burn. The inside of an empty room. Then with no transition the room contains a figure. A man in a coat watches eyelessly from a chessboard head.

In the Rex, the urgent jazz continues.

The figure on the screen might have been a man holding a board in front of his face, even has a hand to the board's base, but there is something in his stillness. Thibaut knows he is looking at a manif.

There is no sound to the footage. A volley of bullets rips into the chessboard-man. Thibaut cries out.

The figure does not stagger but the front of his coat and jacket flower in blood. It drips from the board.

The music is breaking down now. People are staring at the screen. They see a soldier in Wehrmacht uniform, turned slowly away from the camera, in another sunbeam-crisscrossed chamber full of floating dust.

A figure in a white coat enters the shot and prods the soldier. Machinery moves. A crucifix is on the wall. The soldier keeps turning, and just as his features should become visible to the camera, with a smooth transition he is back to facing away again, and still turning, his face still hidden.

"That's the Soldier with No Name!" a woman shouts in the quieting room. "I saw him once." A faceless German officer in a dirty uniform, it walks the city flicking away coins on which are written slogans that turn the heads of German fighters. Currency stamped with sedition. The manif foments renegacy. Now, on the screen, it stands on a platform. It still faces away. You will never see its face. There is a noose around its neck.

A trapdoor opens and the soldier falls and snaps hideously to. The crowd cries out.

It sways. Even in death the manif's face never turns toward the camera.

People are standing. On the screen now there is a priest, not Alesch. A glimmer of a darker chamber, for one instant a huge shape.

"That's Drancy," someone says.

A massive intricate thing is strapped down by many parts. At one end of a dissecting table, a sewing machine, at the other an umbrella. Between them, flickering in black and white, is an exquisite corpse. The third that Thibaut has ever seen. Its head is a great spider, twitching limbs above the body of a well-dressed man. Its legs are amphorae. The manif is snared with wires.

Two men appear, in aprons and surgical masks. They heft a grinder and a chain saw.

"No," Thibaut says, but he cannot issue orders backward through the screen.

The men silently fire up their tools. The exquisite corpse watches with its clutch of eyes. Its spider face tries to scuttle. Whatever holds it holds it well. The men bring their blades down.

The audience in the Rex is shouting. The machines touch where the components meet. Up sprays something too pale, too thick to be blood, as they take the manif apart.

The vivisectionists shove through the impossible body. The exquisite corpse reknits and billows out sawdust or shreds of cotton and the men cut faster, against the recalcitrance of Surrealist matter. Down go the saws.

And the corpse is nothing. Three everyday nothings. Remnants. Inanimate.

To dark. Light. More priests, scientists, someone carrying the parts of another manif. A man nods at the camera—he has no mustache, but Thibaut recognizes the dark-haired man who got away with Alesch.

The film blebs and the man is gone. For seconds there is only light. Then for an instant the screen is full of a new figure, a huge and lurching shadow with a terrible face, coming for the camera.

The Rex is tumult. The image is frozen. There are only those eyes like bowls of shadows, mouth like a tusked hole. It looms.

"That's not a manif," says Sam quietly, startling Thibaut amid the chaos. He did not hear her descend from the booth. "That's a devil. But something's wrong with it."

"How do you know?"

"I know." She hands him a few ends of film, and he holds them up and sees tiny exquisite corpses ripped into their components by machines, bleeding from tentacular toes, back-bent legs or mountain legs or twisted scarf legs, concentric-ring torsos with butter-knife arms, their lolling heads hammer and a sickle or knight's helmet or a pair of bloodied kissing lovers. Exquisite executions.

"We know they're learning to control manifs," he says. They look at each other while the customers of the Rex holler. "The whip for the wolf-tables. The woman on the Vélo. She wasn't on their side but they must know each other's techniques. And now they're using some manifs for *sacrifices*."

"And there are devils," Sam says. "They're building up to something. You saw that man? Just before the last thing? The man from the jeep?"

"Maybe that's Wolfgang Gerhard," he says. "Of the Fall Rot project."

"He might be calling himself that," she says. "But that's not his name. I recognize him and I know his name. His name is Josef Mengele."

"How do you know all this?" Thibaut says at last. He is angry with himself for asking. "What does all this mean?"

Sam speaks quickly as the noise in the cinema increases, the Free French and others shouting about what they've seen. "What it means is some kind of plan. Mengele's a specialist. He experiments. On human life, it was. And now he's come *in*. *In* to Paris, to work with Alesch.

Mengele's not religious! He must need a specialist in devils. They're collaborating. And with the K Commission, too. Manifs and devils and the changing of life."

Thibaut says, "Fall Rot."

"We have to get out of here," Sam says. "Any second now they'll close the door to this place and plan an idiotic, bound-to-fail all-out assault."

"So," Thibaut makes himself say. "Bring help."

He meets Sam's calm gaze. He can see her considering how to respond. No one can hear them in the uproar. "Come on," he says, "stop playing. Just get help."

"I can't," she says.

"You think I can't see you?" he says. "That camera is not a camera. How do you know so much about all this? About the devils. Because you *liked witches* when you were a kid? Come on. You're OSS."

She looks very calm. If she *is* an agent of the American state, then she's the ally of these Free French, and his enemy. Yet here he still is. She needs him for something still, he knows, and perhaps he needs her.

"Special Operations, yes," she says, after a long moment. "That camera *is* a camera. But it has other uses, too."

"You lied to me."

"Of course."

He blinks. "The woman on the Vélo was British, SOE. She was trying to find out about the Fall Rot program, too?"

"There's a lot of us here," she says. "She'd done well. We need to know what this program is. We can't let them proceed."

Thibaut turns from her in disgust and she hisses, literally hisses like an animal.

"Don't you dare," she says. "You *wanted* to come with me."

"What about the book?" he says. He can barely believe his own words. He waits for her to laugh.

But she says, "What about it? The pictures are real. The book'll be real. We're putting together something called the Congress for Cultural Freedom. Perhaps," she says with cold politeness, "you might join?"

"You're my fucking enemy . . ."

"Yes." A spy. He knows she understands him. She knows exactly how he opposes her.

Around them all the factions are gathering. "You heard me," she says urgently. "In a moment they're going to make some stupid plan and probably attack a petty local Gruppenführer, which I suppose is at least a distraction, and they're going to confront *you* and *me* and find out you're Main à plume. Which will not go well. And believe me, you're worth far, far more to me than any of them are. So, hate me as much as you want, and you and Trotsky and your fucking lost Pope Breton and whoever else can bring your worst to bear to bring the whole of capitalist imperialism or whatever crashing down when this is over. But if Fall Rot happens, it'll be over for *both* of us."

"So *call for help,* spy." He should kill her right now. He is sure if he tried she'd kill him first. He looks again at the face still on the screen.

"There's a dampener over this city, even beyond the twenty," she says. "I can't call out. Most of the time no one can. Something's happening, and I need to know what, now. Christ, you have instincts. Are you telling me you can't feel it? And even if I *could* call out, you think it would help? If someone's carrying a bomb you don't disarm it by blowing them up. You know why Drancy's buildings are in a horseshoe shape? They're a *focus*. There've been many, many sacrifices there.

"Alesch and Mengele are calling something up," she says, "and we need a scalpel, not a shotgun."

"I'm no scalpel," he says.

The raucousness and fury in the room are increasing. Thibaut considers terrible plans coming to pass just beyond the arrondissements, in the occupied zone.

"No indeed," Sam says. "But I think I could use *that*." She jerks her head toward the door, toward the exquisite corpse outside. "And it does not like me. And you *want* to go. You want to get out, but not to betray your city. Well, this is your chance to serve Paris by leaving it, Thibaut. So shall we not waste any more time?

"I can't call for backup. For the cavalry." She thumps her own chest and stands taller. Thibaut steps back at the sight of her expression. "That," she says, "is what I am. I *am* what's been sent for."

Chapter Eight

1941

Raymond Couraud smelt of sweat. He scowled in the heat and wiped his thin face on his shirt. He walked fast through country that, he supposed, a person might believe was simply spring fields and roads, little villages, churches, the mumbled greetings of locals. That was not the truth. There were the squadrons of Vichy militia. The border of the occupied zone, where the patrols became those of German soldiers.

Raymond did not know what it was he had taken from Parsons's room. It was contraband, though, something with no business in this world. The trembling little box made his skin prickle and his eyes dry. It had taken next to nothing to push open the door, to watch the American's stupid face wheezing in sleep. Raymond had been gone before dawn. He blew a kiss down the road behind him. *Sorry, Mary Jayne.* Raymond could always sense a thing worth money. He recognized a commodity.

He passed churches, their weathervanes twisting too fast. A dead bird was embedded in the bark of a tree. Raymond knew an offering when he saw one. One night he heard what sounded almost like cows. But there was too much irony in the lowing: something was mimicking cattle. There were things in France now he did not want to understand.

His job was to take this thing, whatever it was, to Paris, and sell it to anyone who hated Nazis. He would go to Britain. He would cross the channel with his money and join the Free French. He would kill as many Germans as he could, and he would do so a rich man.

Paris: swastikas and Germans. Raymond walked past Nazi officers chatting in a pavement café just as if he were a harmless man. He crossed between bicycles under the Arc de Triomphe, watched a woman flirting with a young German officer and imagined killing them both. Shooting the man first, once in the head, then several in his dead body to make it dance while the treacherous woman screamed.

There were not many places more dangerous for Raymond than Paris, but he was not afraid. He paid for a cheap room near the Tuileries. On a burning hot day he entered a chemist by avenue des Ternes and waited seemingly engrossed away from the counter among the packets and powders until the last of the other customers left. He turned and smiled at the shopkeeper.

"Oh my God," the man breathed. "Killer."

"Relax, Claude," said Raymond. "I just need some contacts."

"I don't have any! It's too risky right now . . ."

"Please. I don't believe you. And even if it's true, I need you to get back into it and spread the word. I have something to sell. I'll be at Les Deux Magots. Usual cut if anyone comes through you." Greed took hold of his old contact's face.

"What is it?"

"I don't know."

"Killer," Claude pleaded.

"I don't know. Truly. You know the rumors." He met the man's gaze. "I've been *down south,* man. You know what it's like down there? Now I know there's a market in oddities. Let's not play fools. Ever since those fuckers came, things've . . ." He shrugged.

Since the Nazis. Since their black sun experiments, since whatever it was that was rising started rising. There was a market in books and objects that did not behave as objects should. Raymond had not believed until he saw Parsons's battery.

"Put out the word," he said.

———

For two days, no one came. Raymond was patient. He sat in the café with his wares in a bag. He worked out who were the criminals, the waiters, the artists. The Resistance. Were the inhabitants of the villa cursing him? Doubtless. He felt scornful affection for Mary Jayne.

On the third evening a big man in a painter's smock sat opposite him and asked how much. Raymond quoted and the man got up and left without a word.

He came back the next night, as Raymond had thought he would. Raymond walked through the bead curtain at the rear of the room. He put a bill in a waiter's top pocket so the man would walk away. Raymond waited at the back of the kitchen. Implements swung on hooks. The big man came to him.

Raymond opened his bag. Nestled in scrunched-up newspaper was Parsons's box. The man's eyes went wide.

"May I touch?" he said. Raymond shook his head. Chefs pretended not to see.

"You can see it's something," Raymond said. "I don't know what and I don't care. You want it?"

"I want it," the man said. "Is there room for negotiation?"

Of course there was, of course that was how this always worked. But there was something in the man's hesitation, in the slowness of his answers, the exact tenor of his agitation, that made Raymond say, "No."

There was a commotion from the café. Raymond slung the bag onto his shoulder and the other man looked back at the doorway and Killer knew that he had made a mistake. He had time to wonder if it was Claude who had sold him out, as an officer in dark leather swept the beads aside and entered.

Raymond moved.

Someone shouted, and waiters and cooks started to run. Raymond grabbed his supposed buyer by the hair and yanked him behind a thick spice cabinet.

He heard calls in German and French. The man in his grip wriggled and Raymond smacked him in the face and pushed a pistol into his temple. The box crackled. Raymond Killer Couraud glanced out from behind the cabinet at SS men. There was one in plain clothes. His hands were up and glowing.

"You can't get out," someone called.

Raymond shoved his prisoner into view, pistol to the back of his head. "Shoot and you hit your boy," he shouted.

"We don't want to hit anyone. We just want what you're selling."

The man in the long coat was pouring off light. Raymond shielded his eyes. The man was a tracework of glow, his veins lit under his skin. His hands glimmered. Pots and pans rattled. He crooned and icicles formed on the ends of his fingers. Scum tapping power.

Killer fired. An officer went down and there was a rapid burst of return fire and bullets smashed into the wall and took out his prisoner as Killer ducked back. It was freezing cold suddenly, and everything was out of control, and everything was too fast, and Killer fired without aiming, at where he hoped the glowing man was attempting his bastard invocation.

That box was humming so loudly the bag seemed to sing. It shook. Something soared up and over and there was a thud as it landed inside, nestled by the battery, like a fat apple. *"Nein!"* someone shouted. *"Nicht . . ."*

It was a grenade. Raymond grabbed for it. He scrabbled.

Here came streaking jets of force out of the bad-magic man's hands, power, words, occult light, all mixing with the buzzing box, and the grenade as it began to explode, and in the burst and black-powder and hermetic flare of all of that the stolen battery itself, the pump, the engine full of Surrealist dreams, went up.

Jack Parsons's box became a warhead.

Nothing could hold it.

A blast, an acceleration, the distillate, the spirit, the history, the weaponized soul of convulsive beauty went critical.

It unfolded.

A whimper, a shriek, the burr of insects' wings, the tolling of a bell, a city-wide outrushing, an explosion, a sweep and stream and a nova, megaton imaginary, of random and of dreams. That winnowing wind of Arnaud, of Lefebvre, Brassaï, Agar, Malkine, Aline Gagnaire and

Desnos, Valentine Hugo, Masson, Allan-Dastros, Itkine, Kiki, Rius and Boumeester and Breton and all of them in all the world and all that they had loved and all that they'd ever dreamed up. A fucking storm, a reconfiguring, a shock wave of mad love, a burning blast of unconscious.

Paris fell, or rose, or fell, or rose, or fell.

Chapter Nine

1950

The border of the old city remains blocked with wire and guns. "There's no way we're getting out aboveground," Sam says.

But Mairie des Lilas, the last Métro station on the line, sits a few streets east of the rim of the barrier. Outside, beyond the sealed-off twenty.

Sam descends the stairs at the junction of the nineteenth and twentieth into bad darkness, and Thibaut follows. They walk the tunnels you should never enter. They pass trains that stopped years ago. Through the undercity.

Thibaut breathes shallowly, carefully, his hands trembling. A barrier wells out of the gloom before them. The remains of a checkpoint abandoned back in the first days, when the Germans decided the predators below the pavement were security enough.

Sam has her camera up, and sweeps ahead of them. Behind Thibaut the exquisite corpse follows.

Thibaut watches for monsters. He watches for trains that sit up on their haunches and tell stories.

Something whisks past beyond their torchlight. Sam shouts a command in a terrible resonant voice, in no language Thibaut recognizes, and the thing screams and scurries on, and Thibaut shoots.

It's a little dying devil, a thing like a shrunken man with a shrunken horse's head. Sam's voice and Thibaut's bullets have torn through its weak hexes.

I came low, it is whirring to itself. *To come home. To try to come home, hush, I came low.*

That small demonicide is the only one necessary. Thibaut can hardly believe it. They ascend at last, shuddering, into the air beyond old Paris, with the light flooding his eyes.

It has been a very long time since he breathed the air beyond the arrondissements. It smells of architecture. Thibaut opens his eyes on the roof of Drancy and waits for Sam's word.

This zone has long been evacuated, under rains of bombs. It is far less touched by manifestation than the streets he knows, but more shattered and deserted, quotidian ruin.

They have moved fast, with care and silence. Thibaut's urgency communicates itself, and the exquisite corpse folded space for them a little, so they stalked the miles to Drancy more quickly than they should. Now the sun hauls up. Thibaut and Sam look down at an empty corridor below a cracked skylight.

"You said you saw the brekerman before," Thibaut says. "When?"

Sam glances at him, and looks back through the glass.

"Why me?" Thibaut says. "Why did you bring me?"

"*You* came with *me*," she says. "And that was good, because of that thing." She looks at the exquisite corpse standing like a chimney at the roof's edge. "They've never liked me, manifs. It would never let me get close."

Thibaut looks at the sky. "You've been using me to get to a manif? For whatever this is? Were you looking for someone like me?"

"How could I have been? You came to *me*, in the forest."

"Still, though. I don't know how but you tracked me down."

"Don't give yourself that out," she says. She puts her hands on the slats of the roof. Deep in the building, Thibaut hears a faint wind rushing. "You want to know the truth? The truth is if I could've tracked someone like you down, I would've done. Because yes I wanted someone manif-friendly. Because I wanted a manif. But I was just being chased, and you just came to help.

"You're the Surrealist. You're the one who taps objective chance. You wanted to know about Fall Rot. You wanted to know what's happening. Well, Paris heard you, Thibaut. It was you who found *me*."

She grimaces with effort and the wind below increases.

"What are you doing?" Thibaut says.

"Do you think OSS could have got us out of the Rex?" she says through gritted teeth. "Jesus, it's strong here! You think the *Americans* could have got us through the Métro?" Her hands are not steady.

Thibaut remembers the wind dispersing smoke ghosts on the bridge. Sam's camera is round her neck, but it isn't the camera that's vibrating now, it's her, her sinews stretching in her neck, the scleras of her eyes darkening. Whatever is happening in the building is pouring not out of the camera but through her.

"So you wanted me with you because this thing listens to me," Thibaut says. "Because it could get into the café."

"It doesn't like me," she gasps. "It can smell something on me." She smiles. "I'm secret service, yes, but not American, OSS. That was you who said that. Come on. Not the Americans or the Brits. Nor the French or Canadians or any of them." Her hands flatten into the roof so hard they seem to press into its substance. There is a slamming. In the courtyard below, from all over Drancy, soldiers emerge into the daylight.

"I never gave up that occult stuff I told you about," Sam gasps. "You already know what I'm telling you, Thibaut— you've watched me. And there's nowhere you can go, and nothing you can do. And yes you're my enemy but the Nazis are my enemies, too, more, and they're yours, too.

"Devils and Nazis don't work together well. They *have* to collaborate, they're bound together, there are treaties, whether they like it or not. That's what magic is. And the S-Blast or something locked the gates. I would love to call for backup, as you put it, but the routes are closed, so my employers sent me in. Because I'm from here, so I'm *not* trapped. And I know this world better than any of them."

She opens one hand in front of him, and it's covered in frost, and then in darkness. "I'm black ops, yes, and I'm in deep. Double. I am on the OSS books but that's cover, Thibaut. I work for an agency colloquially known as Bad Marrow. And neither you nor I could ever say its real name, not with our mouths. It's the secret service of the underplace.

"I'm a spy for Hell."

Thibaut and Sam follow the exquisite corpse down smoke-filled hallways. Young German soldiers appear and raise their weapons.

Sam takes two out with witch-blasts, Thibaut a third
with an ill-aimed burst of bullets. His heart shakes him.
The manif ends another attack with a Surrealist assassi-
nation: the man at whom it stares sits suddenly down, un-
does his buttons, looks into his body, now a cage filled
with angry crows, and is still.

I'm working with Hell. Thibaut is giddy, not ashamed.
Does he despise Hell, he thinks, more than he does the
imperialists? Few of the devils want to be in Paris. They
obey the Nazis truculently, where they do at all.

"You're not one of them," he says to Sam. He follows
her through the hallways. He does not ask her why she
might work for these infernal powers.

"Hell doesn't want to risk open war with Germany,"
she says. She glances around a corner and beckons him on.
"A human agent's deniable. There's *something* happening
here, but we don't know what, even beyond the arrondissements, hexes block us seeing."

"Why were you in the city?" Thibaut says. "Why've you
not been here all along?"

"Because of Les Deux Magots. We had to get what was
there. It was a buffoon who thought he was one of ours
who did all this, somehow, you know. In '41. An American
idiot named Parsons. Then a thief called Couraud. We
thought the machine might still be the key." She shakes her
head.

"When was it you saw the brekerman before?" Thibaut
grabs Sam's arm. He stops her in the corridor and makes

her face him. "That head. In your film. And that photo of
the huge arm. And the elephant Celebes *was* there . . ."

"Christ," she says, in English. "Remove your hand from
me. What I saw," she says slowly, "was the brekerman that
killed your teachers. That picture was the aftermath."

"You were *there*? The ambush?"

Thibaut knows what ended Iché and the others now, in
what shape the Nazi onslaught had come. That stamping
marble man, then unbroken. His blood moves fast. "What
happened?"

"To the statue?" Her stare is steady. "Celebes happened. One of the last of your people left alive must have
invoked it, or attracted its attention. It came slamming in
to fight. Just . . . too late. It smashed that brekerman
apart, though. Is that a consolation? You saw what it did."

For a moment Thibaut imagines. The elephant manif
under a microclimate of swirling dark, sending walls
crashing, stamping down the ruins with its four squat feet.
Leaping and whipping with its trunk, rage withering the
Nazi stone.

"Why were you there?" he says.

"It never would have worked," she says, with what is
almost care. "The Nazis knew about it. That's *why* the
brekerman was waiting. They'd infiltrated your cells. It
was an ambush."

"How do you *know*? How did you know to *be* there?"

For a moment she does not answer. "When I was in
the eighth," she says. "In their offices. You asked what

pictures I had that got them chasing me? Well." She shrugs. "I think they think I know more than I do, but I did see plans."

Thibaut is breathing very fast. "For this counterattack? Did you say anything? You said nothing, didn't you? You should have *told* them." His voice rises until he is shouting into her face. "Did you try to tell the Main à plume what was *coming*?"

"I didn't know what was coming, just that *something* would." She is quite calm. "That was the point. I had no time to tell anyone, anyway."

How many times had she said to him she wanted a picture of everything?

"You didn't know what was coming but you *hoped*," he says. "You didn't tell them because you thought it might be this thing that's here, this *Fall Rot*, that came. That you might find out what it was."

"Yes," she says. "I did. There was nothing I could've done to stop your comrades losing their lives in their idiotic attack. The Free French watched, you know that? They were there, too. But they didn't intervene. I couldn't have saved your people even if I'd wanted to but I thought *maybe* I could find out what this 'Secret Invocation' was the documents referred to. Sounded like they were having trouble with it. Imagine my surprise when it was just a manif." Just Breker's vulgarity.

"You let them die!"

"I needed to know what the Nazis had. So I could stop

them. Your *comrades*," she says the word mockingly, "were going to die, anyway. I work for Hell, Thibaut."

Sam clenches her fist and opens her mouth in a sudden wordless shout, and Thibaut hears windows blow out on other floors. He wants to say more but men have appeared in the corridor, again, guards are firing machine guns at the exquisite corpse. It staggers but rallies. It steps through intervening space to stave in their heads. It pushes open a door and, polite as a curate, waits for its companions.

"After this," Sam says, "we can have this out. But now? Shall we?" She indicates the way. Thibaut looks at her, at the flickering light in the threshold.

When after long moments he says nothing, she heads for it, and he follows.

A huge chamber. The center of Drancy has been hollowed into an emptiness fringed by the remnants of pipes and doorways, walls, where once there were bunks and berths, offices, laboratories, torture chambers, before the undesirables of Vichy were moved elsewhere. The room is full of terrible machines.

Panicked scientists and SS officers prod at gauges and dials below an Alesch crucifix. They have stayed behind as Sam's hexes send fires through the building. On one wall above them is a big sigil it hurts Thibaut's head to see.

In the center of the cavernous room priests are circled around a heaving tarpaulin-shrouded bulk. They are linked by chains and wires, a fence of men. They are fervently praying, clicking rosaries.

Beneath the shroud something huge is raging. It howls and moves.

Right below the crucifix Thibaut sees Alesch himself, sees him see them back. Alesch raises his hands in a kind of murderous cringe.

A uniformed man steps forward, pistol raised. An almost boyish face under dark sweat-slick hair, his mouth in a crooked gap-toothed grimace. Josef Mengele. He aims at the intruders and all his Gestapo aim, too.

Sam snaps, her witched camera blasting a man apart. Thibaut raises his own rifle, flexing his innards as hard as he can when he shoots and a flock of owl-headed jugs plummet from nothing to harass the Gestapo.

The exquisite corpse runs at the Germans. The soldiers fire. Their bullets do nothing. Someone shouts a curse. The manif reaches them. It hits with its hammers, breaking Nazi hands and bones and weapons as they scream and shoot it again.

"Take Alesch out!" Sam shouts. "And Mengele!" She scrambles for cover. The exquisite corpse is making for the priests now. "Call it off, quick!" she calls. "Sic it on the fucking doctor!"

And Thibaut shouts at it but the manif has its fury up. He tries to stop it, scrunching up his eyes, but if it hears his unvocalized plea it ignores him. It reaches the circle of prayers.

It leaps as it comes, its legs go stiff, it descends. It tramples a priest.

The man falls and dies. The chains that link him to his fellows snap.

One by one they begin to scream. They stare at their dead colleague. There is the sound of tearing canvas.

"Wait," shouts Sam. "It's broken the circle! Those machines . . ."

"What have you done?" someone yells in French.

From under the shroud, a shell roars out. A line of fire blasts a hole in the wall.

There is silence. Fingers grip the torn hole from beneath. They clutch. Something bellows.

The priests are pulling off the wires that link them, scrabbling to get away. Alesch is shouting, flattened against the wall, and Mengele is running. The thing beneath the tarpaulin grips it and begins to tear. With a wall-cracking cry, the beast uncovers itself, rips itself to light.

Fall Rot.

Caterpillar treads grind. The oilcloth falls shredded to unveil a tank. A Panzer III, stained by conflict, rolls forward on the concrete. From the front of the chassis, in front of the gun-turret, protrudes the torso and head of a giant. A man.

Fall Rot.

He is vast. He wears an outsized German helmet. His skin is cold white, his veins and muscles marked as if by wormtracks. He drips shadows from his eyes. His mouth is full of sharp teeth. He bunches immense arms.

The demon is a centaur of tank and great man-shape. It is festooned with German flags.

"They've made their *own demon*," Sam screams. Absurd as ever, she raises her camera and begins to run right at Fall Rot. Her face is pure hate. "They *built* it . . ."

Made under German orders, by Mengele's biological researches and Alesch's toxic faith, from the broken matter of Hell's natives and from the energies of manifested executed art and their own murderous tech. To be a *loyal* demon, to be made of Nazi triumph. The avatar of the defeat of France.

But their protections were precarious. The encircling prayer is gone, and Fall Rot rampages.

It grabs two crawling priests, one head in each fist. It slaps them together, killing them offhandedly, swings their limp bodies as clubs against their comrades.

It howls in what should never have been a language, spews dirt and exhaust. Sam comes for it, spitting magic.

Mengele hauls Alesch by his robes and screams at him to focus. The room is filling with smoke and rubble and crawling priests and wounded soldiers. The Nazi doctor stands in the construct devil's path. He slaps Alesch's face and points.

Fall Rot rolls toward them.

"*Sie werden mir gehorchen,*" Mengele shouts. Alesch makes some holy sign. Fall Rot winces and swats the air.

Behind that man-shape the tank's gun swivels so the barrel smacks into Fall Rot's pale side. It keeps pushing. "My God," Thibaut whispers.

The devil howls as the metal shoves brutally right into its body. It shatters ribs, rips skin that fountains blood, pushes aside innards and organs and plows on in. The devil screams.

The gun rips right through Fall Rot and the demon's chest reknits imperfectly in its wake, bones jostling back roughly into position, blood drying, skin fusing inaccurately. The weapon sucks free from the other side of Fall Rot's meat with an audible plop.

"*Sie . . .*" Mengele says, and goes silent. He raises his pistol and fires repeatedly into the demon's flesh. He does not miss. Fall Rot keeps coming. The gun turns, dripping Fall Rot's blood. Alesch shouts a prayer, pushes Mengele forward.

The demon laughs and fires. The doctor disappears in a blast of blood and flame and mortar.

The exquisite corpse attacks.

The manif rushes for Fall Rot, clicking in a frenzy, all its hate for the devilish pushing it hard and bringing its transmuting attentions to bear. With a scream of gears,

Fall Rot lurches forward. It backhands the exquisite corpse, sends it spinning.

The made demon and the living art circle each other. The manif stalks, staring with its old-man eyes. The machine-demon swivels jerkily, keeps the art in its sights. Its gun grinds back into Fall Rot's body, making it bay, and the barrel stops midway through the meat, aiming through the sternum.

The manif's limbs are twitching, reaching for energies so the air vibrates. But it has never faced a devil like this. Fall Rot rolls forward, barrel pointing squarely at the exquisite corpse.

Thibaut shouts a wordless warning but Fall Rot does not fire. It looks quizzical. It reaches out and grabs its adversary, one huge long-nailed hand at each of the manif's joints. Those claws tense. The exquisite corpse shudders.

The devil-thing made by science and demonology, built to obey and disobeying that injunction, infernal avatar of an invasion, lifts its face and croons.

With one awful wrenching motion Fall Rot rips the exquisite corpse apart.

There is a blast of energy, a great release. Everyone quakes. The manif's components scatter. The engines whine.

When Thibaut's head clears he looks up to see the devil sucking at the ragged end of the exquisite corpse's head. It licks at the broken machine parts where it tore the art apart. Thibaut retches. The devil laps.

They made this demon manifophagic. *That's the energy,* Thibaut understands. *The fuel is the sacrifice of manifs, that's what kept this secret channel open, so they could grab Hell-flesh and make this. It eats art.*

Fall Rot throws the exquisite corpse's head in one direction, its human legs in another.

Sam calls Thibaut's name. She is wrestling with Alesch. Thibaut staggers toward her. He raises his gun but cannot fire at the bishop for fear of hitting her. They are fighting in the dust, by the gauges and dials. Thibaut feels the shake of tank treads. *Fall Rot is coming.*

He sees Sam stab Alesch with a sharpened tripod leg. The bishop screams and convulses. She gets him to the floor and kneels over him and brings her weapon down again. He moans. She bellows into the camera that protrudes from him.

A radio, too, tuned to an afterlife channel? She reaches up and presses buttons on the Nazi engines.

Fall Rot gropes with its big hands and its big face smiles. Its gun pulls free of its body.

Sam keeps pressing as the demon comes, quick sequences repeated until there is a sudden static crack. "Here!" Sam shouts in English. "It's open! It's here!"

Fall Rot will go loose in Paris. It will eat the manifs of Paris, and grow stronger.

It raises its arms and Sam screams into her camera again, and the room rumbles.

Fall Rot looks down.

A bass roar grows. Louder and higher, it rises with Doppler shift. There's a screaming across the below as if a plane races through great caverns and tunnels, keeps on getting louder and louder until it is unbearable, until Thibaut and Sam clap their hands to their ears and he sees Fall Rot do the same, its expression anguished, and Thibaut feels his insides quiver and something rushes up toward the light.

The flat earth detonates.

A convulsion. Thibaut is thrown back hard in a blaze of shattered stone.

A bomb-blast. A raid from beneath. Thibaut glimpses fire and an explosion billowing up through the earth, an igniting plume, shoving into the tank-centaur, enveloping it in fire, flame that roars up, makes Fall Rot roar, too, in agony it doesn't understand, goes up then stops, a frozen moment of conflagration. A still moment.

Which then as he watches reverses very suddenly and fast, like rewound film, and sucks everything away. Rushes back into the new chasm. Takes the tank-thing Fall Rot rushing with it, into the deep, leaving not a trace. Returns to the pit.

Thibaut lies coughing for a long time. A huge crater slides down into black. There is no tank, no tank-ruin, no too-big human torso visible. Thibaut stands.

A second percussion sounds, a quieter, crackling blast in another room close by, and he cowers. But it is quickly gone and Thibaut rises again.

"I got through to them," Sam whispers. Thibaut's ears are ringing but he can hear her. "This little gate cracked open. I got it wider." With the energies of sacrifice. With what she did to Alesch. "They *had* to come up for this. For that . . . thing."

She leans against a wall. Sparks burst from the machinery. A few researchers are still alive, are moving, crawling in the dust. "That," Sam shouts at them, "was *definitely against the fucking treaties.*"

"You said they . . . your bosses . . . couldn't intervene," Thibaut says. "Or wouldn't."

"There was a block in place. You saw what the priests were doing until the manif . . . stopped them. And my bosses wanted to avoid confrontation. But I got through. And they couldn't let *that* lie. There'll be a serious diplomatic incident."

Thibaut laughs at that a long time, hurting his wound. Even Sam smiles.

They stumble through the ruin while the Germans still alive crawl away from them. When he reaches it, Thibaut hesitates, then picks up the exquisite corpse's head.

It is half as big again as his own, but fleshy and light as papier-mâché. It moves its eyes to watch him, sadly. Some last bolus of life. The train in its beard makes a little *hffhffhff* sound. The caterpillar does not pulse.

They go into the hallway. At the end is a cell containing a pile of terrible objects. Farmyard pieces, a rotting elephant head, leaves, tennis rackets, big-eyed fish, limbs, a pistol, a tiny figurine, a pile of saucepans, a globe.

"Those are all from exquisite corpses," Thibaut says. A charnel heap of components, a grave of ripped-up manifestation. Opposite them is another bank of machines, an engine and a single bunk like a prisoner's. Thibaut's stomach heaves at the smell of decaying image.

"They've been harnessing what bleeds out of the manifs," Sam says.

Three walls are cracked, chaotic. One side of the room is perfectly neat, perfectly, unnaturally tidy. Its window is unbroken, its wall papered.

"I heard another noise from here," Thibaut says. He sifts through the pile with the barrel of his rifle. He probes with his hand and the soft decay of actualized dream fouls his fingers.

Sam smiles and Thibaut does not smile back. He is thinking of the Main à plume who died. He looks at the flawless wall.

"It must have just kicked out a lot of energy when your bosses blew up that thing," Thibaut says.

She says, "It was an abomination."

———

I saved Paris, Thibaut makes himself think. Destroyed a new utter demon. *I saved the world.* He feels flat. Outside, the sunlight hits them differently than it did within the old city.

Is this it? Are they done?

"Where are the soldiers?" he says.

They stagger on, alone and unmolested. They strain to hear attackers they are sure must be coming, but there is nothing. Relieved, confused, straining to stay alert, Thibaut and Sam haul past dirty broken buildings and rubbled corners. They keep their weapons in their hands in these ghost neighborhoods stained by war, wandering, Thibaut realizes, back toward the old arrondissements.

And then abruptly they are in a jarringly perfect stretch of Paris. The loveliest town and houses. Perfect fronts, vibrant colors, crackless. Even the sky seems brighter.

Sam and Thibaut come to a bewildered stop. Where is everyone? And how is this quarter so clean?

The streets are empty, the sun is high, the shadows are small. The streets feel scoured.

Why don't we have to stay down? Thibaut thinks they should be creeping through the shells of buildings. Where are soldiers? He looks at pretty houses without war damage.

"Something doesn't make sense," Thibaut says.

"Really?" Sam says. "Just one thing?"

They walk on a long time. Immaculate undamaged streets. They see no one.

They pass a big hotel. It is picturesque, spotless, deserted.

"The thing is, Fall Rot was already awake," Thibaut says slowly. "Maybe it wasn't him that they were having trouble manifesting. That they were sacrificing things for. They wrote there was something like that, right? That they had trouble with, trying to bring up. But Fall Rot was *already* manifest. Maybe they realized they couldn't make Fall Rot work. Maybe they were even trying to get *rid* of it, but they couldn't kill it. But what if it was something *else* they couldn't invoke. Until Fall Rot was taken down." Sam is still. "By your bosses. You heard that noise. There was a *lot* of energy when Fall Rot died, for sure. Maybe enough, at last, for whatever.

"When you killed it," Thibaut says, "maybe that was like another sacrifice."

He looks into the eyes of the manif head he still carries. "If killing an exquisite corpse feeds Fall Rot," he whispers, "what does killing Fall Rot feed?"

Sam and Thibaut look at each other. Neither speaks.

They begin to run. Through streets that aren't just too scrubbed, too perfect, too empty for these times, but that have never looked as they do now. That do not look real. Thibaut feels like a stain, a smut of dirt.

"We thought it was manifs to feed demons," Sam says. "What if it's the other way? And they've been trying to call up a *manif*?"

Of what power?

They have been experimenting to control such art. Wolf-tables rallying to the whip. The brekerman, obeying orders as it collapsed.

"They've been trying to summon something," Sam says. They hear gunshots. "In secret. And failing."

"Only," Thibaut says, "we succeeded."

On the rue de Paris, running west toward the edge of the twentieth arrondissement, they see at last the rise of the city barricade at the end of this strange chintz. There by the German positions, jeeps, guns, mortars, the ready troops, the city is abruptly chaotic again, grime and imperfection again, smashed apart and becoming dust.

Between them and the waiting Nazi guards, where the walls change, is a slight figure in a brown suit.

The young man walks slowly toward the old city, as if in a dream or a slowed-down film. His footsteps take too long to land. He wears archaic clothes, trousers that balloon out from pulled-up socks. His hair is a strange pale parted black.

Sam has gone quite white. She says, "No." As the young man approaches them, the German troops fire.

And Thibaut almost falls in astonishment because he sees the man unconcerned by any of the bullets that hit him, he sees him look hard at the closest shooter. And where the man looks, a house rises.

Emerging instantly from nothing, clean, freshly painted, fussily rendered, pale, almost translucent. And the soldier, all the soldiers who were where the house is now are just gone. Replaced, with a sweep of attention, disappeared from this scene.

The façades of Paris reappear, as the figure stares, and they are prettier and more perfect than they have ever looked, and they are quite empty.

"It was never Fall Rot," says Sam. "Kill Fall Rot and we *have* called up a manif. Oh dear God. It's bringing a city."

The young man makes it with every look, is reestablishing Paris in pastel outlines, no not reestablishing but establishing newly, a simpering pretense, as it had never been. A cloying imaginary.

"They've found a self-portrait," Sam says.

The last of the Nazi soldiers are scattering before the annihilating gaze finds them. Now the young man is turning slowly back toward Thibaut and Sam.

"He never could paint people," Sam whispers. "He always left them out. Painted everything empty. Even when he drew himself, he couldn't do features . . ."

The figure turns and Thibaut glimpses its faceless face. Empty. A faint graphite sweep where there should be eyes. Blank as an egg. A poor, cowardly rendition, by a young bad artist.

"It's a self-portrait," he hears Sam repeat. She and Thibaut reach for each other, hold each other up in fear.

Thibaut says, "Of Adolf Hitler."

———

And they try to run, and as Thibaut shouts for her and grabs her pack and as the watercolor manif's attention sweeps toward her, Sam moves with more than human strength. She moves to get them away with speed and motion borrowed from her paymasters below. Her eyes flicker and a corona flares around them and she leaps, reaching, straining for the cover of a wall—

—and she slows in her trajectory and lets go of Thibaut as the Hitler-manif turns and eyelessly stares and takes her in and all around her the broken buildings become postcard-perfect in the cone of that regard. And Sam herself freezes. She is in the air and the self-portrait looks at her and she

is just gone.

Gone. Sam is unpersoned. Effaced in the manif's gaze.

Thibaut crawls backward and bites back her name. The street is pretty, and empty of her.

Too slow, too late, he understands that the manif is looking in his direction, now.

He hurls himself into the window of a cellar. As he falls, the glass heals behind him, brittle as sugar, as the Hitler-manif revises history, brings its vision to bear.

Behind the new façade its stare invokes, the rot of war remains. Thibaut still has hold of Sam's bag, and Sam herself is gone.

He climbs stairs and gets bearings fast and pushes out through another window for a side-street not yet in the manif's field of view.

There really is no Sam. In the distance Thibaut can see some last German soldiers, injured and slow. The watercolor manif must glance at their blockade, because it goes, imperfect for the desired scenery. A featureless street appears in its place. As the manif's look takes in the soldiers, they, too, are instantly not there.

A little blank-faced nonentity bringing peace and prettiness, ending the rubble. Where there is discord, there it brings peace. Not even of death, but of nihil. Paris will be an empty city of charming houses.

This is what the Führer's self-portrait proclaims.

Thibaut braces against a perfect wall. He stays out of sight as it passes. He cranes out behind it and aims at the manif. He shoots. He misses. The manif walks on. Thibaut fires again and it ignores him. He wails as it crosses the threshold of old Paris. It brings its terrible emptying picturesquing gaze to his embellished home.

The watercolor will raise a quaint city. And everything will end. The struggles of the manifs, the angry smoke, the muttering walls, the fighters for conviction, the partisans of freedom and the degradation. Human muck, ready to live and die.

Thibaut hears the smacking of lips. In his hand, the head of the exquisite corpse is moving. He can see a pulse in its larva. Its beard-train lets out a little smoke.

The face smiles at him. It looks knowing. It meets his eye.

Thibaut begins to run. He takes the pretty street behind the watercolor, the seer of empty buildings. The manif of the Führer. The face of the exquisite corpse mutters encouragement from Thibaut's grip.

The Hitler-manif stands at the border of the old city. It hears Thibaut and starts to turn.

And Thibaut has no plan. No idea. Just before the deadening, emptying stare hits him, he simply hurls what he holds.

The exquisite corpse's head catches the manif's look in his place and it does not disappear. It flies through the air at the featurelessness. It hits it full on.

Thibaut blinks. He looks down at himself. He is still there. He remains unseen.

The manif is wrestling with a head too large, a head that has fallen over its own. Like a carnival costume. The exquisite corpse's head sways as the watercolor staggers. The mask blocks its eyes. It blocks the unembellishing gaze that fixes the ruins into nothing.

The self-portrait struggles below it and Thibaut can feel the waves of the watercolor's cloying attention. The face of the exquisite corpse winces. It grows translucent. It is almost banished from this vista by the stare beneath. But with a growl, the exquisite corpse screws up its own presence, and stays right there.

There is an unfolding. A shuffling of presence.

Now the watercolor wears some misplaced boot on one foot, a manif boot abruptly appeared. Its head was not chosen by its artist. The faceless manif of Adolf Hitler is randomizing. There is a fluttering, a cascade of options. As Thibaut watches a quick clicking circuit of alternative objects comes into place as the manif's head. Now its legs are not its legs, but a succession of other things, in random stutter. Its body, too. It is becoming a triple figure.

And though he can still see the brown of its original suit and the distinctive and ugly emptiness of its head slip into position repeatedly among the parts that have started to make it up, to concatenate randomly, the flailing manif is no more defined by them than by the fruit, the bricks, the lizards, the windows and lavender and railway lines and endless other things that are suddenly, also, for instants, its components.

It is becoming exquisite corpse. It is remade. It is without artist.

And in its wake, as its wan precision is replaced by that stochastic rigor, that self-dreamed dream, the buildings that it saw into twee perfection are less perfect again. They quiver. Their colors bleed. They are too saturated, their lines are wrong again. They remember their cracks. And then with breaths of stone-dust they are back to ruination, or are not there, or are battered by age, scarred with the stuff of history, again. Paris is Paris.

There is a scream. A swallow. The light changes. The sun scuttles forward, eager to end this day. Thibaut sinks to his knees. He kneels before the entrance to Paris. He bows his head. The city is as it was.

Standing in front of Thibaut, where the Hitler had been, is his exquisite corpse. Tall again. Old-man face, leaf in his hair. Anvil-and-pieces body. It leans—no, Thibaut realizes, no. It is bowing. It is taking leave.

Thibaut stands, too, so that he can bow back.

The exquisite corpse turns and steps politely away from him, over the threshold, into the nineteenth. Where soon enough, the civilians, the partisans, will know that something has happened.

It will not be long before the occupiers reestablish control of these borders. This plan to remake the city has failed, so they will return to their original methods of control, and plot again. Thibaut is outside, alone since the manif looked. For a few hours, at this point, the borders will be open.

The exquisite corpse is turning up boulevard Sérurier. Its body parts flicker like a timetable display, between options. It rebuilds itself: four-part, this time, feet underwater, a woman's legs, a body like some cubist rumination, flattened head, a puckered-lip dream. It walks on, into the city, where it will keep changing.

Thibaut looks east, into streets outside the old city that are no longer sickly perfect but are still, for a while, empty.

He can go almost anywhere. He looks away from the city's heart, for a long time.

And turns back, at last, to the arrondissements he has known since he was a child. Where there is still a fight.

He is wistful, enjoying the air beyond the limits, knowing it will be a long time until he can breathe it again. His way is clear.

There are other cameras in Paris, to find.

The Last Days of New Paris needs writing. Even though these are not the last days, he decides.

Thibaut grants Sam's memory a moment. He wishes her something. *I have a mission,* he thinks. *The mission. Start from scratch, redo history, make it mine. A new book.*

He puts her notebook and her films in her bag. Thibaut shoves it deep into a hole in the brick of the barricade. The limits of the zone. He makes her records, the evidence of treachery and machinations, secret plans, spells and dissenting art, part of the substance of the edge. For someone to find.

The sun picks out the edges of the affected part, the crumble where there was destruction. He waits until he sees bats in the sky. Then, bruised and tired, triumphant and unsure, Thibaut takes a deep breath and steps over the boundary, back into New Paris, the old city.

AFTERWORD

On Coming to Write
The Last Days of New Paris

In the autumn of 2012 my publishers forwarded me a handwritten message. It was from someone of whom I hadn't thought for many years. I'd known her slightly when we were both students at the same institution, though we'd been in different departments. It was close to two decades since we'd spoken. At first I didn't even recognize her name.

Some online searching reminded me, and filled in blanks. When I'd known her she'd been studying art history, and it seemed that she'd gone on to teach the subject at universities in Europe, specializing in modernism. In the late '90s, so far as I could ascertain, she'd gained a small degree of notoriety by putting on a short series of collaborations with scientists and philosophers, something between performances and avant-garde provocations, with titles like "Not River but Estuary: Steering Aurelius Upstream(s)" and "What's Once and What Wasn't Is Still." I could find no details or descriptions of any of these events.

Around 2002 her online trail dried up. She seemed to disappear. Until she wrote to me.

Her message was terse. She'd read an essay I'd written some time previously that touched on Surrealism, and it had reminded her of my interest in the movement. On that basis, she said, she was contacting me on behalf of someone who very much wanted to meet me, and to whom, in turn, she was certain I'd find it interesting to speak. But there was, she said, a very limited window of possibility, "some doors opening only occasionally and briefly."

She gave the name of a hotel in Farringdon, a room number, a date, and time (less than two weeks away), told me to bring a notebook, and that was all.

I'm not certain why I chose not to ignore the message. Curiosity, mainly, I think—I've received a fair number of eccentric invitations over the years, but none with this sense of vaguely aggressive urgency. In any case, after hemming and hawing, rather surprised at myself, resolved to walk away the instant I was made uncomfortable, I made my way to the—faded but not depressing—hotel. I knocked at the given door, at the given time.

To my surprise it was not my correspondent who opened it but an elderly man. He stood aside for me to enter.

He was well into his eighties, but he stood very straight. He still had half a head of hair, and it was not all gray. He was lean and still strong looking, in clean, faded and battered clothes in a very outdated style. He never lost his expression of suspicion, throughout the hours I was with him.

I asked after my acquaintance and the man shook his head impatiently and answered in growling French, *"Ç'est seulement nous deux."* It was just we two.

My French is bad, but much better passive, listening, than speaking, which turned out to be just as well.

I introduced myself and he nodded and rather pointedly did not reciprocate.

He indicated me to sit in the room's only chair, moving his bag from it. I hesitated to do so because of his age but he motioned again, impatiently, so I obeyed, and for most of the hours that followed he remained standing, sometimes pacing, sometimes shifting his weight a little from leg to leg, never losing his restlessness or energy. When he did sit, it was on the very edge of the made-up bed, and rarely for long.

He told me he understood I was a writer, and that I was interested in Surrealism and in radical politics, and that on that basis he had a story to tell me. I allowed that I was, but cautioned that I was by no means a specialist in the history of the movement. I told him that there were many people more expert than I, and that perhaps he and my acquaintance should seek out one of them.

The man gave one of what was to be his rare wintery smiles.

"Elle a déjà essayé," he said. She had tried already. I was, he said, the fourth person she had contacted, in an increasing hurry as, according to that unclear schedule, time grew short. He let that sit a moment. So I was the best that she could come up with, and now it was my job to listen, to take notes, and ultimately to do with what he told me whatever I thought best.

He waited while I organized myself, got my pen and paper ready. I brought out my phone to record but he shook his head so I put it away again. He seemed to chop the air in front of me with his hands, organizing his thoughts.

"Your Paris," he began, "is old Paris. In New Paris, things were different. There was a man in New Paris. He was looking down. It was night. Beyond a wall of ripped-up city, Nazis were shooting."

Thus began thirty-nine extraordinary, indeed—the adjective isn't hyperbolic—life-changing hours. Over their course, uninterrupted by sleep, growing more and more bleary and vague, fortified by crisps and chocolate and water and a nasty wine from the mini-bar, the man told me the last days of New Paris, the story that I have presented here.

He spoke in *passé simple* and *imparfait:* he was never other than ambiguous about whether what he was telling me was a story, though his explanations of the city's quid-

dity, of its history, his descriptions of the streets and landscapes of New Paris, were completely vivid. At times he
would hesitate and take my notebook from me and scrib-
ble an illustration of what he was describing. I still have
them. He was no artist, but sometimes it helped me visu-
alize. And very often it would provoke a memory in me, of
some other image or poem or passage, and I would take it
from him and draw myself, asking him, "Is this right? Did
it look like this?" Sometimes much later I would go back
to my own books, looking for a source I thought I could
recall. Here I've reproduced those of my sketches that he
implied were most accurate.

On three occasions during our time together, he
brought out some notebooks of his own. Battered, an-
cient, blood- and dirt- and ink-stained things. He would
not let me read them in their entirety, but he would show
me certain sections, certain dated entries in scrawled
French, and let me copy out phrases or even other sketches
of what he documented (those last he clearly had not
drawn himself).

The man was an utterly compelling storyteller, but a
disorganized one. I was captivated and adrift. He spoke
with concentration and without hesitation, but—clearly
feeling under immense pressure of time—he went too fast,
and my notes, made in translation, would falter. He told
events out of order. He doubled back on himself to fill in
details he realized he had missed. Sometimes he would
contradict himself, or veer between historical speculation

and seeming certainty. He could be sidetracked and go off on a rumination or explanation of some detail of New Paris that, while rarely anything other than fascinating, was only tangentially related to the story he was telling.

About New Paris itself, he never spoke with anything other than the most wrenching, oneiric specificity. In his descriptions of the time before the S-Blast, of Marseille, of the Villa Air-Bel, he used a different register. Then he was recounting something told to him, something reconstructed, the result of investigations—investigations unfinished and full of holes, that I, dutifully, with much research, would later do my best to fill.

At first the man would be extremely peremptory with any interruption. As time wore on, particularly in the small hours, when I was startled into awareness of myself by the lonely sound of some car or solitary pedestrian from the night outside (we didn't close the curtains), if I raised a hand to ask for clarification, to suggest the source of some manif he described, to query some historical detail, he would listen more patiently. I would ask questions, and he might answer, and our interaction became an interview of excursuses, at times for an hour or more, before returning to the main track of Thibaut and Sam's journey through the ruins of New Paris.

The man never told me his name, and I did not ask him.

He never referred to Thibaut in anything other than the third person, including when he showed me the notebooks. Of course, however, I became certain that Thibaut was he. In these notes, I've proceeded on that assumption.

This was deeply jarring. Because if, I wondered, I believed he was Thibaut, did I believe he was telling me the truth?

Of course it was absurd. But sitting there in that cheap chair exhaustedly listening to the visitor tell me about life-and-death battles, while London's late-night traffic muttered outside, it didn't seem so. It seemed possible, then plausible, then likely. That I was speaking to an escapee from New Paris, describing some old struggle.

Escaped from his place how? Come here why? I couldn't bring myself to ask him. I was too cowardly, or too respectful, or too something, and then the opportunity was gone.

It's hard for me to reconstruct it now, but I think I thought that this was only one chapter. That the story of Thibaut and Sam, and the more partial and uncertain backstory of the Villa Air-Bel, and of how New Paris came to be, was the first part of a longer history; that he would tell me more stories, of the years subsequent, and perhaps details of other places in that art- and demon-fouled world.

But during a second day he grew more agitated, more uneasy, and spoke with more and more speed. He rushed to reach the end of his story, of what were not, it transpired, the last days of New Paris.

When he was at last done with that—his relief

palpable—I allowed myself to get up, to go to urinate for the first time in a long time. I'm not sure, but now I feel as if I remember, from the bathroom, hearing a door creak open, and close again.

In any case when I came back into the bedroom, the man and his satchel and his notebooks were gone, leaving me with pages and pages of my own scrawl, anguish, excitement, deep confusion, and the hotel bill.

I never saw him again. Nor, even with the expensive help of a private detective, was I ever able to track down the erstwhile acquaintance who had introduced us. I had only my notes, and the task with which I'd been—obviously, if unstatedly—left. It's taken much work, but I've tried at last to discharge it here.

What I've written—as those who summoned me certainly knew I would—has been carefully extracted, distilled, and organized as best as I am able from the voluminous notes I made from the man's rush of narrative. In several places, I have filled it out, even sometimes corrected what he said, as the result of my own researches. Again, I'm sure this was my given role.

Perhaps some readers will deem it unseemly for me not to have restricted myself to the most terse and dispassionate, even verbatim, reportage of what was told me. To them, I can only say that I am, more than anything else, a writer of fiction, and both the woman who contacted me and the man who met me knew that. Perhaps they were indeed merely making do, and would have preferred another reporter: perhaps, though, they wanted the story to be told with something of the register of fiction, to communicate a certain urgency that narrative can bring, that was vividly there in the man's exposition. I've called the story "a novella" here, for decorum's sake, and to justify the way in which I've told it. I don't know if they would approve.

I've also appended a section of references. In organizing this report, and to understand even a little of the generative power of the S-Blast, I spent a very long time trying to source the manifs that the man described. Many, of course, were fairly obvious. The derivation of others he told me himself, often explaining that "Thibaut" knew. In some cases I have followed him in making them explicit within the story: others are in the notes below. The origin of a few of the manifs he did not reveal, or perhaps know.

During the course of our conversation, he mentioned many other phenomena and animate manifs, some of which I recognized or later identified, and all of which I recorded in my long notes on the city's history, demonology, manifology, my drafts of an encyclopedia of New Paris. They are not dealt with here, as they featured in his story only as asides. All his offhand descriptions kept me breathless with a sense of how the war- and dream-ruined city must teem. The explorer in New Paris might encounter nudes descending staircases or brides stripped bare, composites in dark lines from Emmy Bridgewater, the nocturnal cats of Alice Rahon. Her mouth and eyes might be stopped up by butterflies, an assaulting echo of *Winged Domino* from Roland Penrose. Her watch could melt. Wilhelm Freddie's mummy-wrapped horse-head figure might come for her; or a ripple-skirted dress from Rachel Baes, or Seligmann's scuttling woman-legged stool; a swan-neck on dancer's legs, manif from Teige. She might watch Picabia's layered people crawl through each other, or see the hauling exhausted rattling red shapes of Eileen Agar's reaping machine. A clergyman could crawl along her path, manifest from the film of Germaine Dulac. She might face Lise Deharme's young girl in tatters. Hunt the spindly animal skeletons of Wols. Pick from trees laden with meat thrust between the paving slabs. Hide from darkly glowing solarized presences from Lee Miller and Man Ray.

The point, I hope, is clear. The streets of New Paris throng.

Of those manifs mentioned in this narrative, there are, I'm sure, many I've failed to identify. If I understand it correctly, it's in the nature of the S-Blast that the bulk of its results are random, or manifest from the work of unknown artists—by which in Surrealist fashion, I mean people. These I could never possibly know. Other manifs I may not have recognized as such during the telling. There were also presences I feel sure derive from works I've seen, but that I've been unable to recall or track down. Someone more knowledgeable about art than I am may fill in the holes.

The literature on Surrealism is, of course, vast—there are far too many excellent books to list more than a fraction. Besides a huge stack of volumes of reproductions, several dictionaries and encyclopedias of Surrealism, collections of its manifestos and texts, a few of the volumes that I found particularly helpful in making sense of New Paris, as it was described to me, and in identifying the manifs, included Michael Löwy's *Morning Star;* Franklin Rosemont and Robin Kelley's edited *Black, Brown & Beige: Surrealist Writings from Africa and the Diaspora;* Penelope Rosemont's edited *Surrealist Women: An International Anthology;* Michael Richardson and Krzysztof Fijałkowski's edited *Surrealism Against the Current;* and Anne Vernay and Richard Walter's edited *La Main à plume: Anthologie du surréalisme sous l'Occupation.*

Just why the visitor and the woman wanted the history of New Paris told I have no idea. I feel it may be germane, somehow, that a good number of the manifs seem to originate in artworks that, in our world, *post*-date the moment of the S-Blast in theirs. What that might say about the relations between our realities—whether there are certain pieces that insist on being born, whatever the contingencies of a timeline, whether there are certain manifesting forces that reach across what might otherwise seem impermeable barriers of ontology, taking or leaving traces—I don't know.

Three weeks after my meeting in the hotel, I was in a café in Stepney considering our encounter. I chanced to look up, straight through the storefront, at a man standing outside, looking through the glass at me. That is, I think he was looking at me. I can't be sure. Food was displayed on shelves in the window, and from where I sat, an apple blocked my view of the man's face. I could see him beyond it, coated and hatted, unmoving. The apple obscured his eyes, his nose, his mouth. Still, I think he was staring at me.

I drew breath at last and he was gone, too fast for me to ever see his face.

Perhaps some understanding of the nature of the manifs of New Paris, of the source and power of art and manifestation, may be of some help to us, in times to come.

In any case, having been told the story of New Paris, there's no way I could not tell it.

NOTES

Some Manifs, Details,
and their Sources

4 **"It's the *Vélo!*"**: The bicycle-woman is from Leonora Carrington's 1941 pen-and-ink work, *I am an Amateur of Velocipedes*. Though Thibaut was scandalized at the sight, in her drawing, Carrington also depicted a rider on her figureheaded machine.

7 **As everyone gathered watched the black virtue**: The phrase "black virtue"—"*La Vertu noire*"—was my informant's. Based on this, and on his description of the presence-filled darkness behind the glass, the chaos of colors in the house seems to have been a manif of Roberto Matta's oil painting of the same name.

9 **There are worse things than garden airplane traps**: Around 1935, Max Ernst painted more than one *Garden Airplane Trap*, landscapes in which vivid, feathery, fungal, anemone-like flowers overgrow broken planes.

9 **Flocks of bat-winged businessmen and ladies**: Winged figures are hardly culturally unprecedented, but the par-

ticular flying bourgeoisie described seem to me emergent from Ernst's 1934 collage, *Une semaine de bonté:* from the Tuesday of that "week of kindness," its figures cut from catalogues and chimera-ed with draconic wings.

9 **mono- and bi- and triplane geometries:** The horrifying colorless aerial shapes that predate like antimatter are from René Magritte's 1937 painting, *Le Drapeau noir.* It's been claimed that the work was inspired by the bombing of Guernica: in the skies of New Paris its manifs seem like remorseless machinic iterations of some Thanatos.

11 **Huge sunflowers root all over:** Though he did not explicitly refer to it, there was something in the scale of the sunflowers Thibaut described and the unease with which he described them that makes me suspect the progenitor of these oversized specimens of what Dorothea Tanning called the "most aggressive of flowers" is manifest from her 1943 painting *Eine Kleine Nachtmusik,* in which a colossal, balefully glowing specimen threatens two girls.

11 **up-thrust snakes that are their stems:** These snake-held, eye-and-heart-petaled plants, the *Lovers' Flower,* were drawn for André Breton ("quite clumsily," he gracelessly reports) by "Nadja," the woman we now know to be Léona Delacourt, and reproduced in his 1928 quasi-novel named for her.

11 **human hands crawl under spiral shells:** Dora Maar's uncanny photo-collage *Sans Titre* (1934) is the source of the shelled hand manifs. In the war notebooks he showed me, Thibaut describes a fishing village of tents below the Quai d'Auteuil. "People dredge with wire, bring up spiral crustaceans that crawl the wet sand slug-

gishly on human fingers and thumbs. Painted nails. The locals boil them. They winkle steaming hand-meat from the shells and eat without cannibal shame."

11 **each shark is hollow-backed, with a canoe seat:** In 1929, the Belgian journal *Variétés* printed the results of several Surrealist games. In "If, When," one player writes a conditional and another, without looking, a main clause, which are then combined into a new proposition. "If," Elsie Houston mooted, "tigers could prove how grateful they are to us," then, the photographer Suzanne Muzard concluded, "sharks would allow themselves to be used as canoes." As in New Paris, it seems, sharks might sometimes do.

11 **the stumps of its struts, forty storeys up:** Just as the Eiffel Tower is the most iconic image of Paris in our own world, so its astoundingly truncated, floating pinnacle is in Thibaut's. In his *Paris and the Surrealists,* George Melly remarks of the tower in passing that during one discussion about "embellishing" Paris, "it was proposed that 'only the top half be left.'" I've been unable to find any other mention of this mysterious suggestion, which clearly cleaved with the dynamics of the S-Blast.

14 **an impossible composite of tower and human . . . a pair of women's high-heeled feet:** The helmeted figure that investigated the young Thibaut appears to be manifest from a 1927 exquisite corpse created by André Breton, Man Ray, Max Morise, and Yves Tanguy.

16 **enervation infecting house after house:** I have not found a specific source in Céline's work for the manif of enervation mentioned. The overall sense described, of course, permeates his work.

16 **Enigmarelle, foppish robot staggered out of an exhibi-**

tion guide: Enigmarelle was a freakish machine figure with ringletted hair and a vacuous wax smile. The Surrealists were fascinated by the "Man of Steel," supposedly created by the American inventor Frederick Ireland in 1904, and popular in vaudeville. They promised it would attend their 1938 exhibition (it did not). What was without question a fake in our world appears to have become, in New Paris, real.

16 **The dreaming cat:** The bipedal cat is manifest from *The Cat's Dream,* an image by Nadja. It's unclear whether the animal is dangerous, constrained as it is by a weight tied to its right leg, and with its tail tethered by rope to a metal ring that, according to Thibaut, floats constantly behind it and above its head like an unlikely balloon.

16 **sagelands, smoothed alpine topographies like sagging drapes:** It took me some time to realize from his description and the areas' odd name that the "sagelands" are places where geography has come to manifest certain paintings of Kay Sage, with their frozen, twisted, melancholy rippling coils and rock forms.

17 **Under one lamppost, it is night:** This isolated outpost of manif night, with its streetlight, seems certainly to be from Magritte's painting series *The Empire of Light* (1953–54).

22 **Jacques Hérold set a black chain on fire:** It was in May 1944, in our timeline, that the journal *Informations surréalistes* was published with a cover by Jacques Hérold: a simple, stark image of a flaming chain.

30 **a dream mammal watches him with marmoset eyes:** Thibaut made no mention of the source of the image of the clawed beast, and I did not think to try to track it

down. But during quite other researches I came across Valentine Hugo's drawing *The Dream of 21 December 1929,* of that year, and it was clear that it was from there that the animal was manifest. The image also includes a drowned woman: it's possible that the prey, as well as the predator that Thibaut disturbed, was manif.

31 **Redon's leering ten-legged spider:** *The Smiling Spider,* with a gurning, almost chimpanzee-like face, dates from the 1880s, in its original charcoal and later lithograph form. Odilon Redon was one of the Surrealists' revered recent predecessors, and more than one of his *"noirs,"* his "black things," have been sighted in New Paris: Thibaut described to me watching Redon's great sky-gazing eye-balloon rising sedately over the smoking ruins of a battle between Nazi soldiers and forces of the Groupe Manouchian.

33 **such prim Delvaux bones . . . prone Mallo skeletons:** Manifs from the work of Belgian artist Paul Delvaux seem to be relatively common in New Paris, in particular skeletons such as those described here, to which, if not as obsessively as he did his big-eyed nude women, he repeatedly returned. To quote the title of his 1941 image, the whole of New Paris could be considered *"la ville inquiète"*—the worried, apprehensive, anxious, unquiet city. The uneasy city. A city also inhabited by other, fitting, trembling bone figures, ripping themselves apart as they lie shaking, reconstructing themselves repeatedly. They are manifest from Maruja Mallo's 1930 *Antro de fósiles—Den of Fossils.*

34 **The Musée de l'Armée is being emptied . . . by curious undergrowth:** Paul Eluard's idea, from *Le Surréalisme au service de la révolution* number 6 in 1933, has clearly

manifested. The "irrational embellishment" he suggested for Les Invalides was that the area "be replaced by an aspen forest."

36 **"They're called wolf-tables . . . Manifest from an imagining by a man called Brauner.":** The most famous iteration of the *"loup-table,"* the "wolf-table," of the Romanian artist Victor Brauner, was the physical object itself that he made, in our reality, in 1947. Whether or not he physically made it in that of Thibaut, too, I don't know, but he had imagined the furniture-beast at least twice before the S-Blast, in his 1939 paintings *Psychological Space* and *Fascination,* which Thibaut appeared to know. As Thibaut mentions, in both these earlier renderings, as in the later sculpture, the predator's snarling head—"screaming over its shoulder at death," as Breton put it—and tail and ostentatious scrotum appear more vulpine than lupine. Breton considered Brauner's wolf-table to be a uniquely sensitive tapping of fear, of anticipation of the war to come.

37 **a barnacled book:** Initially I presumed that the "book that has rested underwater" was Prospero's grimoire, but in later conversation Thibaut corrected me: it is the manif of a 1936 object made by Leonor Fini.

38 **a spoon covered with fur:** The spoon that Thibaut half expected to find often accompanies a similarly furred cup, he said, and is of course manifest from Meret Oppenheim's famous assemblage, sometimes known as *Breakfast in Fur.* A reasonable minority of the spoons left in New Paris are, apparently, now furred.

40 **" 'Those who are asleep . . . are workers and collaborators in what goes on in the universe.' ":** *Géographie noc-*

turne's opening line, which Thibaut quoted, is from Herakleitos. It, along with *La Main à plume*, was printed in 1941.

45 **"Ithell Colquhoun?":** Colquhoun, in our reality, was an unusual and minor artist who had been expelled from the London Surrealist Group in 1940. She retained a lifelong fascination for the occult, particularly Kabbala, and was a member of various magically inclined orders and groups over the years. She was later the author of the odd hermetic novel *Goose of Hermogenes*.

51 **"'Confusedly . . . forests mingle with legendary creatures hidden in the thickets.'":** Robert Desnos's description of the forest dates from 1926, from the piece "Sleep Spaces."

51 **those rushing futurist plane-presences:** Launched with a manifesto in 1929, *"aeropittura"*—"aeropainting"— was a heavily fascist-influenced iteration of second-generation futurism in Italy. It was associated with Benedetta Cappa, Enrico Prampolini, "Tato" (Guglielmo Sansoni), Fortunato Depero, Fillia and Tullio Crali. It offered its quasi-abstraction in breathless service to imagined speed and bombastic propaganda, and to quasi-religious fascist iconography, such as Gerardo Dottori's 1933 portrait of Mussolini, *Il Duce*. It was the frenetic angular plane-presences of *aeropittura* that appear to have manifested occasionally in New Paris.

51 **"Fauves? . . . The negligible old star?":** The fauvism of André Derain, referenced here, was tolerated and, to a degree, celebrated in the Vichy regime. New Paris is home to a few too-bright figures walked vaguely from his images. A short and elliptical six-line poem by Ger-

trude Stein gives its name—and, in New Paris, its un-
pleasant manifest quiddity—to the manif known as the
negligible old star.

54 **A giant's pissoir:** It was Paul Éluard, in 1933, in the collective discussion on the "irrational embellishment" of
Paris, who suggested the transmogrification of the Arc
de Triomphe into a urinal.

55 **a great sickle-headed fish . . . a woman made up of outsized pebbles:** The fish with its huge orange crescent
head was one of many manifs emerged from the vivid
monsters of Wilfredo Lam. The figure of the stone
woman cropped up more than once in Thibaut's testi-
mony. He sketched it for me, and it was from that that I
was able eventually to identify the manif as Meret Oppenheim's 1938 painting *Stone Woman*. And there is,
indeed, something particularly arresting about the simple image, even among so much strangeness. I'm not
able to express exactly what it is. But I think it may lie in
the fact that because we have heard, many times, in
fairy tales, of people being turned to stone, and because
we've seen statues, we know what we think something
called a "stone woman" must look like. But Oppenheim's reclining, resting woman is composed instead,
jarringly, of a handful of loosely coagulated *pebbles*.
We sense their tactility, we know how they will fit in our
hands. But the chop of the water at her ankles shows
that the woman is appropriately tall, and that these
carefully rendered smooth stones are wildly out of
scale. That problematic of scale, as much as the fact
that the woman is rock, is what is so jarring.

56 **the Palais Garnier, its stairs dinosaur bones:** Breton's
suggestion for the "irrational embellishment" of Palais

Garnier, the opera house, was that it become a perfume fountain, and that its staircase be reconstructed "in the bones of prehistoric animals."

56 **Le Chabanais:** The extraordinary and macabre fate of Le Chabanais is manifest from Tristan Tzara's proposed "embellishment" of 1933. Of the famous brothel, he demands, "[f]ill it with transparent lava and after solidification demolish the outside walls." This, horrifyingly, is what has occurred in New Paris, setting around all those within. They are frozen, suspended, staring and unrotting in eternal surprise, like insects in amber.

56 **A vegetal puppet, stringy, composite floral thing:** The vegetal puppets are manifs from a 1938 work of that name by the Spanish-Mexican anarchist and artist Remedios Varo. Twisted, anguished, fibrous and sliding figures against a dark background, here and there they wear faint traces of human features visible.

56 **Celebes:** Max Ernst's 1921 painting, *Celebes,* or *The Elephant Celebes,* is one of the most celebrated and instantly recognizable works in the Surrealist canon. The vast actualization of it—a strange, terrifying quasi-robot elephant, derived in shape from an image Ernst once saw of a Sudanese corn bin—has become one of the most well-known in New Paris. It leaves a trail on its wanderings through the city, Thibaut told me. Where it stops to rest it leaves pools of sticky yellow grease.

57 **The sun over Paris isn't an empty-hearted ring:** The "sol niger," the black sun, sometimes with a hole at its core, is an image borrowed from alchemy and popular with the Surrealists. Max Ernst painted it repeatedly, as part of his "forest" works, in the 1920s.

57 **smoke figures wafting in and out of presence:** Wolfgang

Paalen, the Austrian-Mexican painter, created the semi-automatic method that led to the "fumages" manifest here in the late 1930s, by holding his paper or canvas over a lit candle or oil lamp so the soot and smoke discolored it, moving it so the marks extended into vaguely recognizable shapes. Over these figures of evanescent schmutz he would then layer ink and/or paint, amending, adding details and texture.

59 **"The horse head.":** Thibaut was later to see her photograph of what Sam called "the horse head." It was a tall and sinister robed figure, staring at the camera, fingering a crucifix in its bulky three-fingered hand. As much, he said, as the cast to a head was equine, it was canine, and savagely fanged. I believe this to be a manif from Leonora Carrington's 1941 drawing, *Do You Know My Aunt Eliza?*

60 **Seligmann. Colquhoun. Ernst and de Givry:** The Surrealists had a long interest in divination, the occult, the hermetic and alchemical and traditions of witchcraft. As well as Ithell Colquhoun, among many other figures who exemplify this tradition are Grillot de Givry (whose 1929 book *Le Musée des sorciers, mages et alchimistes* the Surrealists enthusiastically greeted) and Kurt Seligmann, and the inspirations Nicolas Flamel, Hermes Trismegistus, Agrippa and Joséphin "Sar" Péladan.

61 **" 'On Certain Possibilities of the Irrational Embellishment of a City.' ":** The source of so much of the matter of New Paris, the extraordinary questionnaire-style article about the "irrational embellishment" of Paris, "Sur certaines possibilités d'embellissement irrationnel d'une ville" dates, as noted, from 1933, from issue 6 of

Le Surréalisme au service de la révolution. The piece asks, of seven Surrealists, "[s]hould one keep, move, modify, transform or remove" thirty-one varied and eccentrically chosen Parisian sites (though none of those asked give answers for all of them). Those questioned are Andre Bréton, Paul Éluard, Arthur Harfaux, Maurice Henry, the redoubtable Trotskyist Benjamin Péret, Tristan Tzara, and Georges Wenstein. Not particularly widely cited in the English-language literature on the movement in our timeline, it is obvious from his story that in Thibaut's, this piece has become central to the manifestational nature of New Paris.

61 " 'Chemical-blue, twisted machines of jujube-trees of rotten flesh?' ": The description of the manif inhabitants of the forests that Thibaut quotes comes from the Martinican poet and theorist of Négritude Aimé Césaire, from his *Cahier d'un retour au pays natal,* (Notebook of a Return to the Native Land), published initially in 1939, and in expanded version (in our reality), with a fervent encomium from Breton, in 1947. Césaire, in his original, is not merely describing but invoking the ghosts that manifest in New Paris: "Rise, phantoms, chemical-blue from a forest of hunted beasts of twisted machines of jujube-trees of rotten flesh of a basket of oysters of eyes of a lacework of lashes cut from the lovely sisal of human skin."

62 a feathered sphere the size of a fist: The feathered lookers that feed on the sight of Thibaut and Sam are manifs of the 1937 painting *Object-Phantom* by the astonishing Czech artist known as Toyen, after rejecting the name Marie Čermínová, (and, in Czech grammar, the

feminine gender). Toyen's work seems to have had a strong influence on the topography and inhabitants of New Paris, after the S-Blast.

63 **a winged monkey with owl's eyes:** The monkey on the windowsill is instantly recognizable as a manif of the beast crouching at the feet of the semi-nude woman in a doorway in Dorothea Tanning's 1942 painting *The Birthday*.

64 **It stands like a person under a great weight . . . hedgerow chic:** They did not invent the game of "Consequences," but at 54 rue du Château in the late teens or early 1920s, the Surrealists certainly developed it, giving it the name by which we now know it—"Exquisite Corpse." They raised it to a, perhaps the, central place in all their methodologies. Simone Kahn describes the technique and its importance: "On one of those idle, weary nights which were quite numerous in the early days of Surrealism . . . the Exquisite Corpse was invented . . . The technique of transmission was readily found: the sheet would be folded after the first player's drawing, three or four of its lines passing beyond the fold. The next player would start by prolonging these lines and giving them shape, without having seen the first. From then on, it was delirium." "[W]e had at our command an infallible way of holding the critical intellect in abeyance, and of fully liberating the mind's metaphorical activity," Breton said.

There are countless beautiful examples in the archives. Some are simple lines of black ink on paper; some are carefully colored; some are much more complex and time-consuming cut-and-paste works. Grotesque, playful, sinister, combining the iconography of politics, the components of a bestiary, industrial machinery, and dream grammar. The collaborations include the work of Oscar Dominguez, Yves Tanguy, Pierre Naville, Jeannette Tanguy, Gerardo Lizárraga, Greta Knutson, Valentine Hugo, Breton, Max Morise, André Masson, Nusch Éluard, Picasso, Man Ray, Duchamp, and many others.

The exquisite corpse of which Thibaut and Sam became unlikely companions—which can be seen as the frontispiece of this book—is manif of a 1938 composite collage of stuck-together engraved images by André Breton, Yves Tanguy, and Jacqueline Lamba. It stands, a tottering pile of parts, and looks out from below its caterpillar hat with a vatic melancholy.

65 **everyone . . . feels as if they are on the mezzanine of a snake-flecked staircase:** Thibaut was very specific about this anxiousness he felt in the moment described, putting me in mind of Pierre Roy's 1927 or 1928 oil painting, *Danger on the Stairs,* of a large snake descending and crawling, toward the viewer.

67 **They are in rubble full of birdcages . . . a baby's face the size of a room:** The shooting ranges are manifs from Toyen's various drawings of that title, dating from 1939 to 1940, variations of the flat, troubling, and troubled landscapes. All the components and inhabitants of these stretches Thibaut described to me are from these images: the giant baby's head, for example, is depicted in *Tir IV / The Shooting Gallery.*

68 **a storm of birds:** Birds recur throughout Surrealist iconography, and this collective bird mentioned, the dancing figure Thibaut saw in the sky, may be Loplop, Max Ernst's "Bird Superior."

70 **Chabrun, Léo Malet and Tita:** The role of these and

other stalwarts of La Main à plume, the clandestine Surrealist group, is, of course, more dramatic in New Paris (not that it was uninteresting or without incident in ours).

70 **Thibaut had fought the Carlingue once, alongside Laurence Iché:** I tried repeatedly to persuade Thibaut to speak more of his Main à plume comrades but he was resistant, burdened, it seemed to me, with a respect and mourning that muted him for reasons he could not articulate: their death clearly weighed very heavily on him. Particularly Iché's. In our timeline, Iché survived the war and lived until 2007. For reasons I can't explain, including to myself, I did not tell him this.

The manifs he described fighting alongside, that Iché was able to bring forth and direct, come from her poem "I Prefer Your Uneasiness Like a Dark Lantern," published—in our reality—in *Au fil du vent* in 1942. There she writes of "[t]he eagle-headed caterpillar," "the wind-haired eagle," and "the bath of shredded mirrors."

Iché modeled at various times for several artists, including her father, the sculptor René Iché, a resistance activist with the Groupe du musée de l'Homme. In 1940, she was the model for his bronze *La Déchirée*— *The Torn*—a statuette of a semi-naked, blind woman reaching for the sky. This histrionic allegory for France under Nazi occupation was smuggled to London, where it was given to de Gaulle. He kept it on his desk, and it became something of a symbol of the Resistance. In our reality, the statue later disappeared (Thibaut had never heard of it, so its fate in his world I don't know). This was not a great loss to art.

74 **Sacré-Cœur:** It was Breton who suggested, as one of his "irrational embellishments," that Sacré-Cœur should become a tram depot, painted black. He also claimed it should be transported to the northern region of France, the Beauce. This, obviously, did not occur.

74 **a ladder of sinewy muscled arms:** The ladders of thick arms gripping each other, emerging from the earth and supporting each other at each elbow, leaning against walls, are manifs from an ink drawing by Tita, *Les Bâtisseurs de ruines*, printed in *Transfusion du verbe* in 1941. Other aspects of the landscape of New Paris, as Thibaut described them to me, also seem derived from illustrations from that journal—stones like praying mantis claws, a windowed hand growing from the ground, manifs from Aline Gagnaire's illustration in the same issue, for example.

76 **A huge featureless manif woman holed by drawers . . . dolls crawling crablike:** The drawered, headless woman Thibaut imagines Sam considering is from Dalí's 1937 painting *The Burning Giraffe*. That famous giraffe has also, he told me, more than once galloped through New Paris, pouring out smoke, but the huge propped-up women, extruding drawers from their legs and chests, leaves shedding in drifts from the tree-boughs where should have been their heads, are the more dangerous and threatening manifs. Their drawers slide open and shut hungrily.

　　The dolls mentioned are manifs of Hans Bellmer's notorious and grotesque sculptures of young women's body-parts reconfigured into lubricious and frightening formations.

76 **" 'My pajamas balsam hammer gilt with azure.' ":** Simone

Yoyotte, from whose poem Thibaut's pajamas were a manif, was from Martinique. She was a collaborator of the Parisian Surrealist Group before her death in 1933, at the age of twenty-three. More important, she, along with her brother Pierre, was an activist in the Légitime Défense (Self-Defense) group. It was in their journal, of the same name, that this poem was published, in 1932. The group was formed on Rue Tournon in 1932 by the Martinican poets and philosophers Etienne Léro, Jules Monnerat, René Ménil, and five others, including the Yoyottes. None were above the age of twenty-five. The extraordinary, explosive journal, with its uncompromising anticolonial, Marxist and Surrealist interventions, was later to be described by Léon-Gontran Damas, one of the so-called "fathers" of Négritude, as "the most insurrectional document ever signed by people of color."

88 **Trapped in their Marseille hinterland . . . the Surrealists had drawn new suits, a cartographic rebellion:** The origin story of the "Marseille game," the deck of cards that the captive Surrealists created and described to Parsons, is the same in our timeline as in Thibaut's. The full details of the cards and the artists who depicted them were as follows:

BLACK STARS, FOR DREAMS:
Ace; Oscar Dominguez
Genius—Lautréamont, the author of the Surrealist
    favorite *The Songs of Maldoror;* Wilfredo Lam
Siren—Lewis Carroll's Alice; Wilfredo Lam
Magus—Freud; Oscar Dominguez

RED FLAMES, FOR LOVE AND DESIRE:
Ace; Max Ernst
Genius—Baudelaire; Jacqueline Lamba
Siren—the Portuguese Nun, the supposed author of a
set of passionate love letters of the seventeenth
century (now thought to be fictional); André Masson
Magus—the poet and philosopher Novalis; André
Masson

BLACK LOCKS, FOR KNOWLEDGE:
Ace; André Breton
Genius—Hegel; Victor Brauner
Siren—Hélène Smith, the nineteenth-century French
psychic; Victor Brauner
Magus—Paracelsus; André Breton

RED WHEELS, FOR REVOLUTION:
Ace; Jacqueline Lamba
Genius—the Marquis de Sade; Jacques Hérold
Siren—Lamiel (the heroine of the novel of the same
name, by Stendhal); Jacques Hérold
Magus—Pancho Villa; Max Ernst

The jokers were images of Père Ubu, the monstrous
swearing clown-tyrant of the plays of that beloved Surrealist precursor Alfred Jarry. The image chosen was by
Jarry himself.

In our timeline, the designs were published in the
Surrealist journal *VVV* in 1943, in New York, some re-
worked a little. Mostly this was just a matter of tidying
up the images, but there were more substantial changes.

The Ace of Revolutions, for example, became a wheel seemingly balanced on a spatter-pattern of blood, rather than, as in Lamba's original design, a waterwheel *churning* blood. The radical-melancholy and foreboding sense of blood as a *motor* for change was thus, uncharacteristically for the movement, bowdlerized away.

In the reality of New Paris, the cards were never published, though they did, obviously, appear within the city, in card form no less, as immensely powerful manif items, capable of invoking their geniuses, their sirens and magi. Thibaut claimed to me that it is not just the face cards but the aces and number cards that were present in Paris. What *they* manifest, and how, he did not know.

92 **"A lobster. With wires . . .":** It would be surprising if Salvador Dalí's absurdly iconic Lobster Telephone of 1936 did not appear in Thibaut's reconfigured world.

93 **scratch-figures etched with keys:** In the 1930s, Brassaï famously photographed the images scrawled on and scratched crudely into Paris walls. In New Paris, the faces (as they mostly were) he obsessively captured in black and white are live, and full of motion. If, Thibaut said, you put your ears close to the walls, they move their scratch mouths, and whisper to you in a cementy language no human understands.

94 **a great shark mouth . . . smiling like a stupid angel:** This manif is from a text by Alice Rahon, from 1942, in which she describes, at the horizon of the city, "a great shark mouth appear[ing] with the smile of a stupid angel."

94 **It is a sandbumptious:** The sandbumptious is a freakish beast manifest from the work *March 7 1937—4 (Sand-*

bumptious) by the extraordinary Grace Pailthorpe. Pailthorpe, now an obscure figure, was described in 1936 by Breton as "the best and most truly Surrealist" of the British Surrealists (which could be read, admittedly, as damning with faint praise). She had been a surgeon in France during the First World War, and went on to be a pioneer in British psychoanalysis. Born in 1883, she turned to painting late, at the age of fifty-two, when she met the artist Reuben Mednikoff, who was to become her partner (in another overlap between the worlds of the occult and Surrealism they met at a party hosted by Victor Neuberg, a Satanist and one of Crowley's lovers). Pailthorpe and Mednikoff were expelled from the London Surrealist Group in 1940 in a bout of toxic infighting (Conroy Maddox called Pailthorpe an "Ogre") but the spirit of her work clearly remained allied enough in spirit to be made manifest in New Paris after the S-Blast.

96 **the Lion of Belfort:** The Lion of Belfort is one of the Parisian sites irrationally embellished in 1933, but none of the suggestions from the article exactly concord with Thibaut's description here. The stone figures through which Thibaut walked seem, rather, perhaps to be refugees from the "Lion of Belfort" section of Max Ernst's collage novel *Une semaine de bonté.*

99 **the Statue of Liberty:** The semi-living replacement of the—real—statue in the Jardin du Luxembourg is manifest from a grotesque 1934 collage of the Statue of Liberty by Czech Surrealist Jindřich Štyrský.

104 **where the Palace of Justice once was . . . sawdust swirls from the windows and doors of Sainte-Chapelle:** The form taken by the Palace of Justice in New Paris is a

combination of the "irrational embellishments" suggested by Benjamin Péret, who proposed that it be replaced by a swimming pool, and by André Breton, who wanted it replaced by a huge graffito visible from planes above. It was Tristan Tzara who proposed that the Sainte-Chapelle be filled with sawdust.

105 **the squat square towers to either side of its sunburst central window:** The two towers of New Paris's Notre-Dame have been irrationally embellished somewhat as per Breton's suggestion: he suggested they be replaced by glass containers full of blood and sperm. Why the blood appears to be a blood-vinegar mix, and why the towers are silos, rather than the giant bottles of his suggestion, Thibaut did not claim to know.

106 **Arno Breker's looming, kitsch, retrograde marble figures:** Josef Thorak and Arno Breker, the Austrian-German and German "official" Nazi artists, were sculptors specializing in grandiose sinister "Aryana," held to be the antipode of "degenerate," especially "Jewish" art.

108 **Hélène Smith . . . glossolalic channeler of a strange imagined Mars:** The Surrealists described the medium Hélène Smith (pseudonym for Catherine-Elise Muller), the manif of their dream of whom Thibaut's card summoned, as a "muse" of automatic writing. It was in a trancelike state that she would "channel" a deliberation-free scrawl she called Martian script. Thus she described the lives of extra-terrestrials—Martians and "Ultra-Martians," extraordinary manif figures Thibaut also glimpsed on the Île de la Cité.

124 **the Société de Gévaudan . . . in a Lozère sanatorium:** I was eager to hear more from Thibaut about the Société

de Gévaudan, that he mentioned, but he knew little, and seemed not particularly interested. From our-world sources, I learned that this extraordinary collective was centered in the Saint-Alban psychiatric hospital in the region of Lozère, in south-eastern France. Under the experimental leadership of Lucien Bonnafé and François Tosquelles, in the face of the vicious eugenic ideology of Vichy France, a resistance group was formed in the hospital comprising various of the medical practitioners, including avant-garde psychiatrists (later inspirations to what became known as the "antipsychiatry" movement), alongside philosophers (some of whom, such as Paul Éluard, had been close to Surrealism)— and the patients themselves. They seem to have run a clandestine publishing house, collaborated with other resistance groups, organized weapon drops, all while pursuing "institutional psychotherapy" and "geopsychiatry," the therapeutic collaborative integration of patients into the local population. The facts are extraordinary enough in *our* timeline. But of all the untold stories of the world of New Paris, it is about the actions of the Société de Gévaudan that I would most like to know more.

125 **A man in a coat watches eyelessly from a chessboard head:** The man with the chessboard face seems to be a manif of a photo of Magritte taken by Paul Nougé, in 1937. Before its filmed murder, it had been rumored to walk New Paris in its bulky coat, invoking zugzwangs and gambits, turning situations into chesslike occurrences.

125 **"the Soldier with No Name!":** The Soldier with No Name—*der Soldat ohne Namen*—was the persona of

an anti-Nazi German officer under which the incomparable Claude Cahun and her partner Suzanne Malherbe intervened in the war in Jersey. The two artists instigated an extraordinary campaign of propaganda among the Germans stationed there, distributing flyers and coins painted with anti-Hitler slogans into soldiers' pockets and through their car windows. The soldier, as manifest in New Paris, was said to flick such coins at all who saw him, bringing, or perhaps legitimating, a spirit of mutiny and anti-war resistance particularly among the German forces. It is no wonder it was one of the targets of the Nazis' investigations.

127 **tiny exquisite corpses ripped into their components by machines:** Judging by the descriptions of the exquisite corpses being experimented upon, the Nazis of Drancy had captured specimens manifest from specific collaborative works by Man Ray, Miró, Yves Tanguy, Max Morise, Picasso, Cécile and Paul Éluard, and others.

162 **"It's a self-portrait." . . . "Of Adolf Hitler.":** Of course we cannot see a work by even a twenty-one-year-old Adolf Hitler free of the shadow. We cannot and should not try. The sense of horror that infects the viewer of the future Führer's amateurish watercolor is ineluctable. "A Hitler," we read in the bottom right corner of the image. "1910." A Hitler indeed.

In our timeline, the painting from which this manif occurred was found by Company Sergeant Major Willie McKenna, traveling with comrades in Essen in 1945. According to Thibaut, it has remained unknown in the world of New Paris. It's not due to any particular fame that Sam and Thibaut were able to tell what the manif was, to recognize it.

I've come to think, rather, that they could do so because it is so very accurate a portrait.

A stone bridge straddles a stream. The waters are rendered in dilute red. Perhaps meant to be reflections of sunrise or sunset, it's quite impossible now not to see that river as a tributary of blood. Sitting at the furthest point from us on the bridge, ungainly in a child's pose, his legs dangling over the water, is a figure in brown clothes.

The artist has penciled a cross above it, and—anxiously, pathetically—written "A.H." That is all. There is the sweep of that familiar side-parting, and below it, nothing. Bar hesitant lines for eyebrows, the face is faceless. Unmarked by any features.

The watercolor of young Hitler by young Hitler has no specificity. It is blank. Incompetence makes it a death-drive's dream of itself, in pale skin.

ACKNOWLEDGMENTS

For all their help with this book, my deepest thanks to Mic Cheetham, Julie Crisp, Rupa DasGupta, Maria Dahvana Headley, Simon Kavanagh, Jake Pilikian, Sue Powell, Julien Thuan, and Rosie Warren. I'm very grateful to all at Random House, in particular Dana Blanchette, Keith Clayton, Penelope Haynes, Tom Hoeler, David Moench, Tricia Narwani, Scott Shannon, David G. Stevenson, Annette Szlachta-McGinn, Mark Tavani, and Betsy Wilson; and all at Macmillan and Picador, especially Nick Blake, Robert Clark, Ansa Khan Khattack, Neil Lang, Ravi Mirchandani, and Lauren Welch. For countless formative games of what I did not yet know to call exquisite corpse, my love and thanks to my sister, Jemima Miéville, and the memory of my mother, Claudia Lightfoot.